# The Rowland Sisters, Book 1: Mr Harding Proposes

**By Catherine Dove**

Writers Exchange E-Publishing

http://www.writers-exchange.com

# Chapter 1

"It is hopeless," said Mr. Harding irritably. "Do stop fussing, Elroyd."

His clipped accents made his annoyance sound worse than it was, but his valet had been in his service for many years and was not cowed. "You are not yet beyond hope, sir. Allow me."

Mr. Harding's response was something like a growl. From the chair on the other side of the room, where Mr. Harding's best friend, Mr. Frederick Winborne, was comfortably ensconced, came an amused chuckle. "Not yet beyond all hope? That is lucky, Richard. And to think I had about given up on you."

Both the valet and Mr. Harding ignored him. Elroyd said, "Sir, this is going to be a most important day for you. On this of all days, you should look your very best."

"I should just forget the whole idea."

Mr. Winborne grinned. "Cold feet already? You haven't even left the house, never mind proposed to the chit."

"It is easy for you to sneer." Mr. Harding turned to his friend, pointing a finger. "You wait until some girl gives you a leveler, and then I will get the chance to sneer at you. I will be able to do better, in fact, since I have no doubt you will make a bigger fool of yourself than I." The valet clucked reprovingly at him, and he turned back to the mirror. "Blast. I might just change my mind and go fishing instead, after all."

Elroyd's lips pursed in disapproval. "We would all be disappointed if you did so, sir."

"Oh, you would, would you?"

Correctly attributing his master's snappishness to a case of nerves, Elroyd said evenly, "I think I can safely speak for the rest of the staff in saying that Miss Rowland is a fine young lady whom we would be pleased to serve."

They knew her well enough, too, Mr. Harding reflected. Georgiana had run tame in Five Oaks almost since she had been old enough to run at all. He had helped to raise her, although he was only eight years her senior. His had been the hands to place her on her first horse's back, and it had been he who taught her to drive to an inch. He had been the person called on to partner her in her dancing lessons, and his had been the honest opinion she had sought on her sketches. However, whether this long familiarity would be a help or a hindrance to a proposal of marriage, he had no idea. Georgie was unpredictable, even to him.

He looked at himself in the mirror and sighed. He could see nothing about himself to induce Georgie to accept him. Yet he was generally considered an eligible match. He was of a good Sussex family, was quite well off, and at eight-and-twenty could be thought to be stable in his habits and inclinations. He had inherited his ancestral home of Five Oaks and a small but elegant town house in London on the unexpected deaths of his parents several years ago. He was an excellent whip and a light-handed rider, and had a fine stable that included several carriages. His vices were few, did not include gambling, and were all done in moderation.

His manners were not always agreeable, true, for he had a sardonic sense of humour and an occasionally acid tongue. Still, he was received everywhere, and was quite popular with hostesses because he never arrived late nor left early, nor refused to dance with a girl who had been introduced to him simply because she might be plain. And on the plus side of his mental ledger, Georgie actually found his sarcastic wit funny, and often joined with him in enjoyment of caustic observations on their neighbours and the polite world in general.

On the negative side of the ledger, he was no Adonis. He was not ugly, exactly, but there was no denying that his fair hair tended to the unruly rather than the picturesquely curled, and his features seemed too large for his narrow face. He had good bones, his mother had always assured him, but he would have preferred if those bones had limited themselves to his strong jaw and high forehead, and not added an overlong and aquiline nose to the mix. Even his eyes, grey and well-shaped and definitely his best feature, were overshadowed by heavy brows. As for his mouth, it was far too wide. He was not petty enough to envy the good looks of his friend Mr. Winborne, since that young man's undeniable handsomeness had as much to do with his open, candid good nature as any blessings of birth, but a little of Winborne's evenness of feature would have been helpful.

Still, Georgie had been looking at his face for the past twenty years, and it had not frightened her away yet. And his figure (while again suffering in comparison with Winborne, a noted Corinthian) was trim and broad-shouldered, with a good leg that showed to advantage both in the usual country garb of boots and fawn-coloured breeches, and also in the pantaloons and Hessians or the formal breeches and stockings that were *de rigueur* in town.

He was honouring this occasion with a mulberry coat made by Weston, which he knew set him off at his best, and into which Elroyd was now trying to squeeze him. This task accomplished, Mr. Harding was ready. Elroyd smoothed a wayward wrinkle on a sleeve and bent to rub away an infinitesimal speck of dust from the shine he had put on his master's boots. Then master and valet looked at each other in a moment of male commiseration. "Well," Mr. Harding said. "Wish me luck."

"I most sincerely do, sir."

"Freddy?"

Mr. Winborne jumped to his feet and offered a hand. "Good luck, old chap, and all success." He then clapped Mr. Harding on the shoulder. "Buck up! You look as if you are floored already, and you have not so much as given a jab."

"Do not drink all the brandy while I am gone," Mr. Harding said dryly. "I will need it, win or lose."

The Pink Bedroom at Rowland Hall, domain of the younger daughter of the house, was in utter chaos. Open bandboxes and trunks were scattered about, in the process of either receiving or disgorging their contents. Gowns of muslin were laid out across any appropriately-shaped piece of furniture, as well as all over the bed, obscuring the pretty rose-embroidered coverlet. Bonnets, trailing their ribbons, were tossed on top of the gowns. Across the floor, small satin slippers jostled against boots of kid and jean in no particular order.

Into this disarray strode Miss Georgiana Rowland, to stop and stare about her, the expression in her dark eyes one of wrathful astonishment. "Puddles! What is the meaning of this? We leave in an hour!"

The lady thus addressed, Dorothea Puddleforth, winced at being the target of Miss Rowland's wrath. But she was not fearful of being dismissed on the spot, as someone might who had not, like Miss Puddleforth, been with the family for nearly twenty years. She had originally been brought to Rowland Hall to be nanny to the infant Georgiana, but she had made herself so useful, in many more ways than just as a nanny, and was so willing to learn new tasks, that by the time Georgiana entered the schoolroom, she was prepared to take on the position of governess, with a corresponding rise in salary. But that had not been the limit of Miss Puddleforth's ambition or skills, and now, with her salary doubled, she was Georgiana and Cecilia's very superior dresser.

However, none of this meant that she was always equal to the task of keeping after both girls at all times. Now, standing upon no ceremony, she threw her hands into the air in defeat and despair. "Miss Cecilia has been helping me."

"Helping," Georgie repeated.

"I was just filling the last trunk when Miss Cecilia became convinced that I had left her pink gauze ball gown behind, which naturally necessitated an instant unpacking of several trunks." Miss Puddleforth drew breath. "*Despite* my assurances that the gown was indeed packed and in the largest trunk."

Miss Rowland glanced at the largest trunk and saw a wealth of pink gauze tossed over its open lid. "I see it was found. Or was it unearthed?"

"It was unearthed from precisely where I said it was. However, Miss Cecilia then bethought herself of several other items she considered of absolute necessity."

Laughing, Georgie held up both hands in surrender. "Enough. So where is she now?"

"In the attic, looking for pink velvet ribbon that she swears will exactly match the ball gown that I did *not* forget to pack."

Georgie's face registered instant and rueful understanding. "Dear me. Was I this much trouble to you when I went to London for my first Season, dearest Puddles?"

Miss Puddleforth's stern face softened at this. "No, you were not, and you know it."

Georgie grinned. "I am sure I was not, for I recall leaving all the packing in your capable hands and not lifting a finger to help."

"Which, if I may say so, is exactly what Miss Cecilia should do."

"Has Mama not told her we will be buying her a proper wardrobe, all new, when we are settled in town? I am sure she has!--for I recall Cecy's raptures. Why, then, does she think she will need all these gowns?"

"I am sure I do not know," Miss Puddleforth said ominously.

Georgie stared all around her. "Never mind. I will send Cecy to the Dower House with a basket of fruit for Great-Aunt Honouria, and while she is there, you will pack exactly what you think needful. When she asks about any particular item, simply say it is packed, and do not tell her that it is packed right back here in her room, where it belongs."

"And when she wonders how I managed to get everything into one trunk?"

Georgie was a girl of mercurial moods and a keen sense of the ridiculous. With this dry comment, her frown cleared and her merry giggle broke out. "When she does, I will marvel at what a model of efficiency you are, and swear that you did just the same for me!"

Miss Puddleforth smiled grimly at this, then set back to work, sweeping up an armload of gowns from the bed to be transferred back to their original places.

A footman at the door bore a summons to attend her mother, so Georgie left Puddles, content that now at least one part of the packing would be done smoothly. Georgie's own packing was already finished. A natural inclination toward organization and the experience of three Seasons made her efficient, even when she had surrendered Puddles' services to Cecy for the time being. She knew she could count on Miss Jericord to have her mother's trunks at the door no more than an hour or so later than the planned time of departure.

But there was still discord for her to face, because her mother, who would never dream of contradicting her very superior dresser, did not have the same reserve about Rowland Hall's butler.

Riddle, grown old in the deceased Lord Rowland's service, had never completely relinquished control of the household to his master's widow. Lord Rowland had been a bachelor for so long that most matchmaking mamas had given up on him. By the time he had suddenly fallen madly in love with Miss Maria Becknall, some twenty years his junior, married her, and brought her home, Riddle was quite set in his ways.

Lady Rowland's and Riddle's conflicting ideas about what was absolutely necessary for a few months' stay in London always provided much entertainment for the girls and their elder brother Charles, who had succeeded to his father's title on Lord Rowland's death some years ago and was now living in town. Georgie herself tended to side--tactfully--with Riddle on most issues, and never more than in their annual removal to London. Still, she could not help but wish, when she came downstairs to find the entrance hall as chaotic as her sister's bedroom, that the butler could find some other way of protesting his mistress' folly.

Riddle's method was crude, but effective. He would set out every single thing Lady Rowland considered essential, then stand back with a lugubrious expression, letting her see the sheer impossible volume of it and allowing her to make her usual half-hearted and disorganized attempt to sort through it all. Then he would gracefully, if somewhat smugly, accept the charge she would lay on him to do the best he could with it. Georgie knew that Riddle would eventually whittle the enormous mess down to something manageable, but, with a sigh, she acknowledged to herself that she would have wounded feelings to soothe yet again. There was no chance they would arrive at the Red Lion any earlier than seven in the evening. She had bespoken rooms, and the inn was long accustomed to Lady Rowland's fits and starts, but that did not make Georgie any more comfortable with forcing the inn's servants to wait up late and be put to such additional trouble.

# *Chapter 2*

Georgie found her mother in the South Drawing Room, alone, clutching her vinaigrette in one trembling hand and a delicate, lace-edged handkerchief in the other. "There you are, Georgiana," wailed Lady Rowland. "Where have you been? How could you wander off like that, when you know things are such a mess? Riddle will *not* do as I tell him, no matter how often I explain why something must be done or not done. You must speak to him. He will listen to you. Although I do not know why, I am sure, when after all he is *my* butler."

"I will speak to him, certainly, Mama," Georgie said ambiguously.

"And what of Cecilia? Have you seen her?"

"No, Mama, not since breakfast." She refrained from mentioning that Cecilia had spent the past hour frustrating Miss Puddleforth.

"Wretched child!" her mother said, meaning Cecilia. "You would think she would be excited about leaving for London at last."

"I am sure she is."

"After all, has she not been begging me to bring her out ever since your first Season? Not that I could have, since she was not even out of the schoolroom, but you see what I mean. I have been wanting her any time this past hour, but can I find her? No!" She clutched her handkerchief to her breast. "Why is it that removing to London always creates so much trouble? It never did when your father was alive. My nerves cannot take much more of this, Georgiana. I have already had a spasm, and my head *aches* so!

And it is so difficult, launching a girl into the ton. You girls simply do not realize the effort involved! Not that you are any trouble, my dear, and, indeed, I am almost glad that you have never married, so that you are here to help me. But I simply do not understand it!"

"Understand what, Mama?"

"I do not understand why you are still on the shelf! It is not as if you are plain, for you are not! Nor are you dowerless, like poor Amelia Bagnold--for which we can thank Henry as much as your father. My brother is so kind to us! What we would do without him, I do not know. We would have to rent a house, for one thing, and that would be an enormous effort."

Since Georgie knew that this task would have fallen on the family lawyer or, perhaps, Uncle Henry himself, she was able to refrain from sympathizing.

Her mother, despite wandering freely about in her conversations, never forgot her original tack, and she went on, "Nor is there anything wrong with your birth. A Becknall can look as high as she pleases for a husband, and it is not nothing to be Miss Rowland of Rowland Hall. It is not as if you have had no offers, either. Scores of them!" she added with considerable exaggeration. "I can understand why you did not accept young Bibberley, who has those unfortunate spots, or Evercoll, who has not a feather to fly with, and all because of his addiction to gaming. But why did you not marry Lord Averley when he offered for you? So respectable a man, and an earl, too!"

"And five-and-forty years of age, with three daughters," Georgie said calmly, accustomed to being taken to task on this subject.

"Indeed, I had forgotten the daughters. The eldest is your age, as well. He has a mistress, too, and I cannot think he'd give her up after all these years, so perhaps it is just as well. But what about that nice Mr. Fotheringhay? Pray, what was wrong with him? Only four-and-twenty, quite a respectable portion, and so handsome! Such good manners!"

"And no conversation."

"I found him wonderfully conversable."

Georgie stifled her immediate response, which would have been highly unflattering to her parent, and instead retorted, "Very well, *you* marry him."

"You will always be joking," her mother said severely, "but I cannot comprehend why you keep turning down every offer of marriage you receive."

"It is very simple, Mama. I have not yet had an offer from a man I thought I could live with for the rest of my life. In fact, I have not had an offer from a man whose company I could tolerate for more than a few hours."

"I know what it is," Lady Rowland said shrewdly. "You are waiting to fall in love, which is the most nonsensical thing in the world."

Georgie, who did have something of the sort in her mind, said with a tinge of sadness, "Did not you love Papa?"

"Of course I loved your father! But when I married him, I hardly knew him. My own father chose him for me. Naturally I did not find him repugnant, or my father would not have advanced the match. But we were practically strangers when we wed. I grew to love him afterward, and it was a fine marriage we had, too. All these romantic notions come from novels, not from real life. I always knew you read too much." A sudden thought made her sit up straighter. "I do hope you have not put the same ideas into Cecilia's head! As much as I love her, I must admit she does not have your common sense, my dear, and girls like her always fall in love with the most *unsuitable* men! Not that there is any harm in it," she said in an abrupt about-face, "as long as you do nothing improper, and do not break your heart, for it is quite natural to be falling in love at your age. But marriage is something different. I would never want you to marry a man you could not like, but, dearest, you are much too particular. You have to marry *somebody*, after all."

"Do I?"

"Well, of course. What else would you do?"

"I have a perfectly respectable portion of my own. I can set up my own establishment, with Puddles to give me countenance."

Her mother let out a little shriek. "Please, do not say such things! Why, you'd be an outcast, an old maid, a... a hermit!"

"Very well, Mama. We shall not talk about it anymore." But Georgie knew that someday her handsome and popular brother would eventually decide to take a wife, and on that day, she planned to be out of Rowland Hall, wherever she had to go.

No, when Charles married, she would be gone, as far away from Rowland Hall as she could get. With none of this determination showing on her face, however, she said, "Why did you send for me, Mama? Did you want me to go find Cecelia for you?"

"No! I want you to talk to Richard."

"About what? He has already agreed to stable our horses."

"I meant, talk to him now. He is here."

"Richard is here? He has been waiting for me? Why did not you tell me?"

"I am sure I would have, if you did not keep interrupting me. He came a few minutes ago. Riddle was busy elsewhere, who knows where, and he just let himself in past the footman, so I told him I would summon you. Honestly, I am sorry to ever say anything to the detriment of the Squire and Lady Harding, God rest their souls, but they raised that boy with no manners at all. He is a disgrace. He simply thrust his head in here, asked where you were, and disappeared again, without so much as a how-d'ye do or inquiring after our healths."

Georgie resisted smiling. "Yes, Mama, I am aware that he is the rudest man in Sussex. Where is he now?"

"I am sure I do not know. He runs so tame about the place, he could be anywhere. Ask Riddle. Riddle thinks he knows everything," she added, her tone descending from complaint to acidity.

# Chapter 3

Georgie made her escape and found Riddle in the foyer, looking over the chaos with a jaundiced eye. The butler did, indeed, know where Mr. Harding was. "I put him in the Library, Miss, as I could not answer for how long you would be."

"Did you serve him some refreshment?"

Riddle's expression was a rebuke. "Yes, Miss."

"Thank you. I will go to him there. Thank you, Riddle. Oh, and Riddle-- my mother is having a spasm, so we should be able to move forward with the packing now."

"Thank you, Miss. I shall see to it," the butler said with awful dignity, and turned to those of his staff who were currently in the foyer, all of whom became instantly attentive.

Feeling half-hysterical and fully harassed, Georgie went to the Library. There she found her childhood friend amid the litter of several stacks of books on the floor, one of which had tumbled over, either from its own weight and lack of balance or from the careless brush of a passing leg. "I see Cecy has been here, too," she sighed.

Mr. Harding was perched on her father's large oak desk, one booted leg swinging idly, a glass of brandy beside him, a book in one hand, and an expression of sardonic amusement on his face. Just the sight of him made Georgie feel better, and she threw herself into the chair opposite him. She need stand on no more ceremony with Richard than she did with Charles, and in fact regarded him in the light of an older, wiser brother.

When her father died, shortly after having accomplished the goal of seeing his heir sent off to his own school of Eton, the part of a masculine presence in Georgie's life had been filled both by her beloved Uncle Henry and by Richard, primarily the latter, since Uncle Henry lived in London year round. Her father had provided her with this library, but Richard had been the person with whom she'd discussed what she read. Lord Rowland had provided her with prime horseflesh, but it had been Richard who'd thrown her up on her first mount, shown her the best way to take a fence, taught her to drive to an inch, and warned her of the perils that awaited a well-mounted and adventuresome girl in the Sussex countryside.

Nor had he abandoned her when she passed from her hoydenish youth and become a dashing young woman. When she had gone to London for her first Season, Richard had been her comfortable escort until she found her feet, and she had never feared being without a partner when attending a party or ball to which Richard had been invited.

He responded now to her unorthodox greeting by giving an exaggerated start of surprise. "Cecy, here! I did not think it! I am certain that you and Sir Henry are the only readers amongst the Rowlands. In fact," he mused, "I suspect there is a divine law which states there can only be one intellect per generation in your family."

She scowled at him. "Cecy is not uneducated."

"But the education does not seem to have altered her mind much. Has that girl *ever* opened a book, except to hide a love letter in one?"

"Richard! Cecy's never gotten a love letter."

"I was speaking rhetorically. What has you so up in the boughs?"

She gaped at him. "Did you not come through the entrance hall?"

"Certainly. Did you think I climbed in the window?"

"You have done it before," she pointed out.

"Not since I was twelve! But why is all that mess fretting you? Riddle will clean it up. He always does."

"I know, but I wanted to be at the Red Lion for dinner, and we shall never make it now." She sighed, then gave him her attention. "What did you want that would not wait until we got to town?" Alarmed at a sudden thought, she said, "You *are* going to London, are you not?"

"A pretty fix you'd be in, if I were not."

"I would be." Uncle Henry, who kindly housed and fed the family during the Season, did not keep a carriage and had converted his stables to storerooms, so Georgie had gotten into the habit of stabling her horses with Richard. "Then why are you here?"

"Actually," he said casually, setting aside the book, "I came to see if you wanted to marry me."

She stared at him, then burst out laughing. "So you can take me away from all this?" she said with a broad gesture.

"Would you not like to escape?"

"Infinitely, but I need not get married to do it!" she said, still bubbling with laughter. "It is a princely gesture, Richard, truly, but I do believe that, between them, Puddles and Riddle will get us on the road sometime today, without any more undue effort on my part. So you see, I do not need rescuing, even by such a charming means."

"Then marry me because you love me," he suggested.

She wriggled her feet, which hurt, and teased him back. "I love you far too well to marry you, dearest," she said, looking up at him with a mischievous twinkle.

He folded his arms on his chest and regarded her with a mixture of irritation and fond amusement. "Then marry me because I love you."

"Of course. As soon as I want to get married, I shall inform you of the fact. Now, please stop joking with me and tell me why you are really here. I have to find Cecy, who has disappeared to some unimaginable region of the house, and I still have a thousand other things to get done."

He gazed reflectively up at the ceiling. "Well, if you will not marry me..."

"Will you please be serious?"

"If you insist. I wanted to tell you that I will send Bloomsbury and some of the boys to fetch your horses tomorrow, so that is one thing you need not arrange. They can bring them by easy stages with my own cattle."

"Thank you so much!" she said with genuine gratitude. "Will not you be needing Bloomsbury, though?"

He shook his head. "My curricle is being repaired."

"Repaired? You did not overturn it, did you?"

He was offended, and she immediately apologized. He then deigned to explain, "I am getting the springs reworked, and I think one of the wheels has warped slightly, so I am having it replaced. Another thing I meant to ask. Have you a copy of that book your uncle wrote? The one that was just published? Because you know he is going to ask me if I have read it, and I have not so much as looked at the binding."

"Yes, of course. It is in this mess somewhere," she said, looking vaguely about her. "The servants must have decided to dust in here today. How inconvenient."

"Do not worry, I will find it. Since you refuse my most generous proposal, I shall take my wounded heart away, consign you to your chosen fate, and let you go about your business out there in the hall. I think I shall leave by the window. I am in disfavour with your mother. Again."

# Chapter 4

Mr. Harding made his escape, not by the window, but by a side door. Not so much as the quiver of a muscle in his face revealed to the groom holding his horse that his errand to Rowland Hall had been anything but the most ordinary, nor that it had been accomplished to anything less than his satisfaction. However, once he was clear of the village proper and navigating the lanes that led to his own home (if one wanted to go tamely and without jumping fences and walls), he let the gloom within his heart appear on his expression. His bay hack, sensing its master's distraction by the relaxing of his seat and hands, slowed to a lazy amble and even, briefly, considered stopping to crop the tempting greenery that was springing forth on the trees and ground around him. Although Mr. Harding had enough presence of mind to nip this minor rebellion in the bud, he paid little more attention than to be sure the animal was on the right path. His mind was focused on finding some way to accept his defeat with some dignity.

A fair man, he did not place the blame for his failure on fate or bad luck, but on himself. Despite being often corrected by his parents, he'd never bothered to put a check on his tongue or on the acerbic wit natural to his nature. Although in society his manners were acceptable, while he was amongst his friends, he'd indulged his freakish sense of humour and love of the ridiculous, and Georgie had always been counted in the number of his friends. He had gone to Rowland Hall prepared to be made happy, or to be rejected, but what had never occurred to him was that he would be assumed to be making a pleasant joke to enliven her day and ease her mood. Yet, she was not being unreasonable, as this was something that he might have done, when in the right humour.

He was certain that no man of his acquaintance, or even knowledge, had ever been *laughed at* while proposing marriage, but he'd laid that ground himself, and now must bear the weight of it.

His sole consolation was that he had been able to preserve enough dignity and aplomb to avoid letting Georgie see how her laughter had cut him. He had been afraid that, with rejection, he would have lost the free and easy friendship that the two of them had always enjoyed. He had at least been able to avoid that particular tragedy.

*Tragedy,* he thought with a wry grimace. *No tragedy, but a farce.* He was sure that, after some time had passed, he'd be able to smile at this thought. After twenty years, perhaps.

In the way of all households, although he had enjoined Elroyd to strictest secrecy and was certain his valet had not betrayed his confidence, every servant had somehow become cognizant of his mission to Rowland Hall. Or so he guessed when his head groom, and not one of the stable lads, came forth to hold his horse for him to dismount. Bloomsbury's expression was discreetly hopeful, but instantly fell when seeing Mr. Harding's grave aspect. Too well-trained to comment, he contented himself with silent commiseration as he led the bay back to the stables. Mr. Harding, brushing specks from his coat, resigned himself to the prospect of receiving such commiserating looks from all his servants for some time to come.

A measure of the seriousness with which his mission was regarded was that he found his valet instead of his butler serving his guest brandy when, with Sir Henry's new book under his arm and (metaphorically speaking) his tail between his legs, he entered the drawing room. Both Mr. Winborne and Elroyd looked at him with even more blatant expectancy to wish him happy than had Bloomsbury, and both read the answer in his face at once. Elroyd blurted, "Never tell me she refused you, sir!"

"Not exactly," he said dryly, sitting opposite Mr. Winborne and placing the book negligently aside.

Mr. Winborne grabbed at some fragment of hope. "She needs to think about it, is that it? That's perfectly natural. Women always do that. They like to keep a fellow dangling for a while."

"Not exactly that, either. Ah, thank you, Elroyd." He cradled the brandy snifter in both hands, stared into its depths for a long moment, then drank deeply. "She laughed at me," he admitted. Speaking it aloud, even if only to his best friend and to his valet, hurt fully as much as he had expected.

Elroyd looked grave, but Mr. Winborne sat up in shock. "She never did! Why, that would be cruel, and if there's a cruel streak in that girl's nature, then I have to say, she had me properly fooled."

"She did laugh. The circumstances were... not propitious. She jumped to the conclusion that I was joking with her."

Mr. Winborne's eyes went round and his brows climbed. "You must have said it very badly."

"Thank you for your confidence," Mr. Harding sneered. Then he admitted, "Actually, I could not have phrased it any way to make it acceptable. I picked the worst possible time. I am appropriately punished for my procrastination. I know better, too. When they leave for London, too much of the true work descends upon Georgie. She was harried, and there was no opportunity to talk at any length with her and explain that my feelings toward her have altered."

"But you did actually propose," said Mr. Winborne, whose intellect, while not lacking, was also not powerful, and who liked to have everything neatly laid out.

"I did, but only because I had sworn to myself that I would not leave without doing so."

"Now, wait." Mr. Winborne's pleasant face screwed up comically as he pondered. "She did not actually refuse you, is that right?"

"I would consider receiving a proposal with laughter as a refusal, myself," Mr. Harding drawled.

"No, it is not! She is not set against you, old chap! She just has not gotten out of the habit of thinking of you as a brother, is all. You went about this backward. First you have to convince her you love her, and then you propose."

"Again?"

"Do not give me that expression. You will not put me down with a mere look and one word. Yes, again. When she is better prepared. And when would be a better time than while she is in London? Wonderful town, London. Balls, breakfasts, theatres. Plenty of opportunity to romance her."

Mr. Harding would have delivered his optimistic friend a stinging set down, but unexpectedly, his valet entered the fray. Elroyd coughed discreetly. "If I may have permission to speak, sir, Miss Rowland is possessed of a ready sense of humour, and she is accustomed to being... jocular, with you. But I am quite sure that she holds you in the highest regard, and that once you have convinced her that your feelings are sincere, she will cease to see your proposal as a joke and accept you."

Mr. Harding stared from one of them to the other. "London or no London, just how am I to do that while she is swamped in all the madness of launching her sister into the ton? In fact," he added in some despair, since he was not and had never been in the petticoat line, "how am I to do it at all?"

Neither his friend nor his valet, both bachelors, had a ready answer to that question.

# Chapter 5

Georgiana Rowland was a young woman with the happy knack of being contented wherever she found herself. If in the country, she enjoyed the slower pace of country life, the beauties of nature, the thrill of hunting, the pleasure of knowing everyone she met at an assembly or ball. If in town, she loved the variety of sights, the constant activity, the culture, and the pleasure of meeting new people at gatherings of all kinds.

The only problem between country and town was *traveling* between them. An easy and hardy traveller herself, she had little patience with the slow pace that Lady Rowland demanded. Even less did she have patience for her mother's constant flow of complaints. When at home, these slid off her, for there were always places to go and things to do. But being confined with her for hours in a closed carriage amplified the irritation, and it took all of Georgie's strength of will not to scream by the end of the first two miles.

Long ago, she had tried various tactics to stop the flow. She had encouraged her mother to try to sleep. "Sleep!" cried Lady Rowland. "How can anyone sleep while being jostled so? How can you be so insensitive as to think I could possibly rest at all under these conditions? In fact, I have a headache, and shall probably get no rest all night. I can never sleep on such a journey anyway. Even when in a bed, I can still feel the jostling. And speaking of beds, the sheets at even the best inns are not properly aired. You scoff at me bringing our own linen, but trust me, if I did not, we would all have colds by the time we reached London."

Georgie had tried reading a book, hoping that by doing so, she'd encourage her mother to fall silent. This, too, was less than successful. "How can you read while in a closed carriage? I assure you that I cannot," vowed the woman who only opened a book if it was a popular novel, and then only until she had learned enough to be able to talk about it at her next ton party or visit. "I am invariably made quite dizzy and ill if I try. I am amazed you are not, but then, you have your father's constitution. Nothing ever troubled him."

When Georgie vouchsafed no response, but went back to her reading, there was a silence of perhaps half a minute's duration, at the end of which time Lady Rowland said, "That must be a fascinating book, to keep you so absorbed. Do you have enough light to read by? It is so closed up in here, I am amazed you can see the print at all. I wish we could open the windows, but then, of course, our clothing would be quite ruined by the dust."

Georgie had, naturally, attempted to reason with her mother on the subject of traveling, but only the very first time, when she'd been quite young. To each of her measured, logical, rational arguments, her mother had a counterargument, and since Lady Rowland was unhampered by a need to be either logical or even rational, Georgie inevitably came out the loser, usually out of the simple frustration of reaching a point where she at last recognized the futility of her attempt.

This particular trip was in some measure improved by her sister's company. Normally, Cecy was as poor a traveller as their mother, but her excitement over her debut in London had made her disregard such inconveniences of the trip as rough roads, poor food, and a room which, despite being at a respectable posting house, would be declared by Lady Rowland to be positively damp. Cecy entered into her concerns about all these things, but most of her attention was absorbed by the wonders of her approach to London. So the conversation in the chaise went something like this:

"Oh, Mama! Have you ever seen such a fine day! Look how the sun is shining!"

"Yes, so it is. Perhaps the road will not be too rough, since it has not yet rained. But the dust will be dreadful. My dear, I know that it is too warm, but please do not venture to open a window. Not that you would, of course. Still, the heat will be terrible by midday. I shall be prostrate by the time we arrive."

Cecilia, blithely ignoring the bulk of that discourse with a facility that Georgie could only envy, promptly said, "Look! Coming up behind us! That must be a phaeton! He is coming so quickly! I think he means to pass us by!"

"It is a curricle," Georgie said, "and he most certainly does mean to give us a pass."

Lady Rowland started. "Oh, tell me that's not so! Why, I am sure there's a corner coming up soon! What if he crashes into us? We could be overturned or driven into the ditch. He might frighten our horses, and they'd run away."

"Mama," Georgie said patiently, "I am sure Tom Coachman will allow none of that to happen. You see? He is making way for that young man to go by."

Cecy observed with awe, "He must be an exceptional driver. His coat has dozens of capes."

Watching the curricle speed past them, Georgie observed, "No more than a dozen. But anyone can have a coat made, Cecy, with however many capes he wishes, and you will find that many men who consider themselves top-rate fiddlers, and who wear an ostentatious number of capes to their coats, are actually far from being able to imitate the perfection they boast.

That particular man, however, does handle the reins in form," she added fairly.

Lady Rowland delivered herself of a long dissertation on the habits of wild young men in general and of those who drove the roads without care for the safety of others in particular, and went from that to a more prosaic complaint of the dust kicked up by the curricle's team. She was just reaching the end of her discourse, as evidenced by her attention straying to the way Cecy was wrinkling her dress by wriggling around to see everything, when her speech, Cecy's raptures, and Georgie's absorption in her book were all brought to a halt by a change in the speed of their carriage. It slowed; it stopped; it rocked slightly as Tom Coachman and the footman jumped down from their posts. "Whatever can be the matter?" demanded Lady Rowland. "Why have we stopped?"

"I will discover the cause," Georgie promised.

She opened the door, and the footman ran to let down the step and hand her out. "You will want to watch your step, Miss. The road's muddy in places."

"I will be careful." Lifting her skirts an inch and treading carefully, she went to the front of the carriage, where she found Tom and the postilion bent over, examining the hind leg of the inside wheeler. "Oh dear. Has he gone lame?"

Tom grunted an assent, his attention on the horse, a lapse in manners that troubled Georgie not a whit. After a short time, he lowered the animal's leg to the ground and said, "It's nought serious, Miss Rowland, it's a stone bruise, but he can't go on, poor brute."

"Of course not. How close is the nearest village?"

"There's Alderbridge, up the road a piece, mebbe a mile, mebbe two. He can make it that far. If her ladyship will consent to wait at the inn there, although it's not what she's used to, I'll send the boy to the next posting house for a change, and we can get on. Won't cost us more than a few hours. Less, mebbe."

Georgie sighed, but there was no help for it. She stepped back into the carriage and informed her mother of the accident, then had to listen with what patience she could muster to her mother alternating between blaming Tom for not being more careful, then the horse for injuring itself, followed by fussing at Georgie for having muddied her boots and the hem of her petticoat.

# Chapter 6

The Golden Cock in Alderbridge was indeed not what Lady Rowland was accustomed to, but it was still a respectable place, consisting of two stories under a steeply pitched roof, and having a substantial yard. To their surprise, there was already a traveling chaise in the yard at the time, a fine equipage laden with baggage and bearing a discreet crest on the door. This vehicle crowded them somewhat, but the ostler, a burly, bustling, but courteous sort of man, assured them he would be able to accommodate their needs.

The owner himself came out to greet them, wringing his hands in nervous pleasure at receiving two members of the Quality in one day. He was able to provide rooms for them, he informed them, but when Lady Rowland said, "We shall not require rooms, just a private parlour for an hour or two," he was dismayed. His private parlour, he explained, had already been taken by the lady who had arrived some half hour before them. Affronted, Lady Rowland exclaimed, "Surely you do not expect me to expose my young and innocent daughters to a *common room*, do you?"

The landlord's face crumpled in dismay. "No, indeed, my lady, I wish no such thing! That thought would be the farthest from... it's not to be thought of! But the lady who arrived before you has explicitly expressed a desire for privacy, you see."

Lady Rowland did not see.

The landlord, at a stand, his hands wringing even more agitatedly, said, "If you would consent to wait here for just a moment, I will send up to see if the lady would object to the company of other females of quality."

"Please do so, and at once. I am about to faint from the heat. This room is so stuffy. And do you never sweep the floors?"

Sped on his way by this adjuration, the landlord bowed and turned, but he had no sooner put his foot on the stair when a maidservant appeared, coming down. "Mr. Nutford, sir, the lady says...begs to inform you, that is, that if the ladies who have just arrived are in need of rest and refreshment, sir, she will willingly share the parlour, and be glad for the company." She bobbed a tardy curtsy at the Rowland party at the end of this rushed, obviously memorized message.

Georgie said, "That is most kind of her. Please tell her that we accept her generosity with great pleasure, and will join her at once."

The maidservant scampered back upstairs, and the landlord bowed deeply in gratitude. Lady Rowland pulled her shawl more snugly about her shoulders and said, "I do not know why she would not do so. Landlord, my daughters and I need something to sustain us."

"Yes, ma'am, naturally, ma'am! I'm sure the wife will find something suitable. If you would just come this way...?"

The parlour that he ushered them into was a fine one, with a sunny southern exposure, polished floors, an adequate board, and enough chairs and to spare for their party. The lady who had hired it, sitting by the windows, rose to greet them as they came in. She was a tall, graceful woman, her age somewhere between Georgie's and Lady Rowland's, dressed in the height of fashion in a gown and pelisse of a subtle green, edged with black lace and buttoned with knots of satin thread. Her hair was striking, of that glorious red known as Titian, dressed high to fall in curls around a truly lovely face, and the eyes that studied them with reserve but also a willingness to accept them were as green as grass. Georgie was instantly impressed by her handsomeness, her mien, her fashionable gown, and most of all by the intelligence and lurking humour in those fine eyes.

However, she should have known that her luck on this day was bound to be uniformly bad. Beside her, her mother stiffened. "Lady Shipton," she acknowledged, but in tones that held more loathing than courtesy.

The lady's faint smile did not waver. "Lady Rowland, is it not? It seems you had an accident to your carriage?"

"Yes. Most unfortunate."

Georgie was astonished by her mother's cold voice, and said at once, "We are most grateful to you, Lady Shipton, for allowing us to share your parlour. I am sure it is an imposition."

"Not at all," the lady said, with much more warmth. "How could anyone with a particle of sensibility allow you to stay downstairs? Please, make yourself comfortable."

"Over here, girls," Lady Rowland ordered, taking the chairs furthest from where Lady Shipton was standing.

Georgie's astonishment at this rudeness was not shared by Lady Shipton. Instead, with a rueful smile, she said, "I see my horses are being poled up now, so you shall not have to share the parlour after all." She placed upon her brilliant curls a smart hat with an open brim and a crown circled by a single ostrich plume, both dyed to exactly match her pelisse, and bent to pick up a Norwich shawl, a pair of kid gloves, and a tiny reticule. "You will find the food here to be better than appearances may indicate, and the lemonade would be an excellent refreshment for your... daughters?"

Lady Rowland performed no introduction, but simply nodded. This time even Cecilia, who had been silent in admiration of the lady's toilette, was startled out of her reverie to stare at her mother.

Georgie stepped in hastily, making a quick curtsy and saying, "Yes, ma'am. Georgiana and Cecilia Rowland."

The lady's eyes met hers, and what passed between them was a swift but clear communication. Georgie knew at once that the lady was quitting the room only to avoid embarrassing her and Cecilia, that she not only bore no ill-will to Lady Rowland but was finding the situation wryly amusing, and that she understood Georgie's situation precisely. "I do hope the rest of your journey is unattended by further inconvenience," she said, speaking to Lady Rowland but looking more at Georgie.

When she was gone, Georgie turned to her mother. "Mama, whatever possessed you to treat Lady Shipton with such discourtesy? After she was so obliging to us!"

Lady Rowland said indignantly, "I would not have had you meet that woman for anything. She is..." But her next words, on which both of her highly curious daughters waited breathlessly, were kept within her motherly bosom. Instead, she said stiffly, "She is not a proper person for you to know. In fact, you will forget this entire incident. If you should meet her anywhere, and she should presume to greet you, you will pass her with no more acknowledgement than a nod."

Georgie and Cecilia exchanged glances behind their mother as she regally went to a chair rather nearer the table. They were tacitly agreed that, while they would not disobey their mama, they had every intention of discovering who Lady Shipton was and why Lady Rowland felt it necessary to do everything but give her the cut direct.

Even as the girls shed their bonnets, the landlord ushered in a maidservant bearing a light repast. Lady Shipton had not deceived them about the quality of Mrs. Nutford's cooking, and they accompanied an excellent meal with lemonade for the girls and a sherry, which Lady Rowland pronounced acceptable. When they had eaten, Lady Rowland dispensed herself in the room's most comfortable chair and at once fell asleep, leaving Georgie and Cecilia to move to the window to enjoy a comfortable chat.

# Chapter 7

The windows of the inn looked over the yard, and gazing out, the sisters got a surprise. Quite half an hour had passed since Lady Shipton's departure, but her chaise was still there, although her horses were now poled up and she was about to step into it. She had been stopped, however, by a gentleman in a drab driving coat, who had swept off his hat and was bowing to her, taking the footman's pleasure of handing her up, an offer she accepted with a faint smile and a regal inclination of her head. He talked to her for a moment, then stepped back and gave the coachman the signal to depart.

Cecilia observed, "Is that not the gentleman with the curricle who passed us earlier?"

"He could very well be. Yes, see? That is his team of chestnuts, I am sure, being led by a groom. They were not here earlier. He must have come back this way."

"He is very handsome," observed Cecilia.

Georgie allowed this to be so. The man was not young, but still in his prime, with a head of dark curls, a good pair of wide shoulders under his coat, and an excellent leg. He glanced up at their window, and Cecilia ducked back, giggling. "Did he see us?"

Georgie, who had positioned herself with a care that he would not, said acerbically, "He certainly saw *you*."

Blushing, Cecilia said, "I never thought he'd look up. He seems to be a friend of Lady Shipton's."

"An acquaintance, at the very least."

"I wonder if that means that he is not quite perfectly respectable."

Cecilia was at the age where "not respectable" was equivalent to "interesting", and Georgie, who had seen more than one of her London acquaintances cast down by the lures of a rake, quickly dampened this speculation by saying, "I daresay he is perfectly respectable. He is quite old, for one thing," she said, perjuring herself without qualm, "and he does not drive neck-or-nothing, but precise to a point, both of which are in his favor. Most likely his acquaintance with Lady Shipton is simply due to them moving in the same circles."

Cecilia glanced at their mother, then turned back to Georgie and wondered, "Why do you think Mama dislikes Lady Shipton so much?" Her eyes wide, she added, "I know Mama is a high stickler, but I have never seen her come the ugly over someone as she did just now."

"I am sure I have no idea why, and I do not think it a good idea for us to speculate."

"Do you think she could be one of those wives of society for whom marriage is simply a facade, meant to allow her to have *affaires*?"

"Cecilia! Where did you ever get a thought like that?" Cecilia did not answer, but blushed, and Georgie made a shrewd guess. "You got it from those novels you have been borrowing from Sophia Yardley, did you not? Honestly, Cecy, while I know I have always encouraged you to read, I meant to *improve* your mind. With books from our own library, not the lending library."

"Oh, stuffy books! I only read those when I cannot go to sleep at night, and need something to make me drowsy. I know that all that is exciting in the novels cannot be true. I am not a child. But still, there *are* women like that in society, are there not?"

Georgie reluctantly conceded this was so. "But I do not rank Lady Shipton among them. She does not look the type, nor was there any indication of flirtation in her greeting to that gentleman, despite his obvious charms."

Cecilia picked up on the relevant portion of this. "Have you *met* women like that?"

"No, of course not! Mama would never be so careless as to allow me to be presented to a woman of... immoral character, no matter how great her rank." She then conceded, "But I have had them pointed out to me, and truthfully, no matter how well they are dressed, they do not contrive to look quite ladylike. Yet Lady Shipton was every inch a lady."

"She was. I would like to look just like her. Did you notice her hat? Have you ever seen anything so prodigiously elegant?"

Georgie welcomed this diversion, never more glad that Cecilia (whose attention had been for nothing but clothes and parties since their mother had informed her that she would make her come-out this Season) was much more interested in Lady Shipton's hat than her reputation. Whatever Lady Rowland's objection to her, baseless or not, she would not be pleased to know her daughters had been discussing the lady.

In a piece with the rest of her luck, however, this, too, was bound for a crash. Lady Rowland awoke an hour later, certain she had only dozed for a moment, and Cecilia blithely asked her if a gown such as Lady Shipton's was suitable for her first Season. Indignant and infuriated, Lady Rowland said it most certainly was not. "If I have told you once, I have told you a hundred times, Cecilia. Only white, and soft blues, pinks, greens, and yellows are proper. And I would not have you copy That Woman in any way, regardless."

"But, Mama, she seemed perfectly ladylike."

Lady Rowland stiffened. "That is a prime example of what I have always told you, that appearances can be deceiving. You cannot judge a person by the way they are dressed. Mutton can dress up as lamb. And appropriate manners can deceive even more. They can be aped by anyone, and by a woman like that, with all her experience, without any effort at all!"

Georgie privately thought that Lady Shipton had acted as she had from a genuine kindness, not from a desire to ape good manners, but kept her tongue between her teeth. Cecilia had no such rein on her own tongue. "What do you mean, her experience?"

"Never mind," Lady Rowland huffed, disappointing both girls. "I do not wish to discuss That Woman for another moment. You will not mention her again, not to me, not between yourselves. I am your mother, and I know The World, and I tell you, she is not a proper person for you to know. You need not understand more." She arranged her shawl about her person, and fretted, "Whatever shall we do for the next few hours? We should have brought something from the carriage with which to entertain ourselves."

"Mama, I told you before, you have been asleep at least an hour," Georgie said.

"Impossible!"

"Then I think you will find we are able to leave much more swiftly than you anticipate."

# *Chapter 8*

Georgie's prediction being fulfilled, they were able to leave within the hour, a time spent by the ladies most agreeably when Mrs. Nutford thought to send up some volumes of *La Belle Assemblee*, sadly worn and outdated, but still a source of pleasure, particularly to Cecilia, who could see herself in all of the elegant gowns pictured before her. Her raptures were dampened when her mother and sister united to declaim them as unsuitable for a girl just coming out, and Cecilia vowed she could not wait for her second Season. To this, Lady Rowland cried, "I hope you will have no such thing! Pray, Cecy, do not be like your sister, forever turning down proposals of marriage for a ridiculous scruple!"

Assured that, once she was married, she would be allowed and even encouraged to wear the gown she admired most, with its Russian bodice and gauze overdress all buttoned with pearls, Cecilia assured her mother she would do no such thing, but would marry whoever was most eligible. "If he is young and handsome, that is," she added thoughtfully.

Their footman, Ned, was ushered in shortly after this to announce that a new wheeler had been procured and the chaise was ready to continue on its way.

To expect to make the same good time to the Red Lion as the post boy had made, on a fresh horse with only a rider to hinder its speed, was not in Georgie's hopes, and indeed the sun was setting when they finally pulled into the yard and were greeted by the familiar ostler. As they tread toward the door of the inn, from which the landlord was already emerging to greet them, Georgie noticed that a team was being poled up to a curricle, a team she thought she recognized. Sure enough, just as they were about to enter the inn, a gentleman stepped out, the same man they'd viewed from the window at the Golden Cock.

He was obviously about to set forth, bound, Georgie thought bitterly, for London, where in his equipage he would easily arrive in time for supper, and was setting his hat at a rakish angle on his head when he saw the Rowland ladies. The hat was immediately swept off, and he gave them a low bow. "Had I known a sight of such beauty was awaiting me, I would have emerged from this inn long ago," he declared.

Cecilia giggled. "If you had, you would have missed us."

"So I would." His smile, as well as his voice, had great charm. "In the absence of the appropriate company, I beg leave to introduce myself. Neil Dandridge, at your complete service, ladies."

Lady Rowland introduced herself and her daughters. "But I believe we have met before, Mr. Dandridge," she observed without enthusiasm. "Are you not related to the Dandridges of Leicestershire?"

"The younger son," he admitted, "and I am overjoyed--and surprised--that you remember me."

"I recall you being a good dancer," was all Lady Rowland would say. "I have not seen you in town these past years, however."

"I was most disagreeably detained elsewhere." At her enquiring look, he said, "In the Army, ma'am."

Georgie glanced at Cecilia, who was watching Mr. Dandridge raptly, and could only be grateful that he was not in full regimentals. Even a plain man in his regimentals was difficult for a girl to resist, and Mr. Dandridge would have been handsome enough in a red coat to fill any young girl's dreams.

On Lady Rowland's enquiring, he admitted, "I have sold out. With the war over, there's little chance for advancement now. I am presently enjoying a period of leisure, although to tell the truth, I am finding it dreadfully dull. Or I was until just now. May I dare to hope that you ladies are on your way to town?"

Lady Rowland acknowledged this to be so.

"I will not be so bold, on such a short and informal acquaintance, to ask if I may leave my card at your residence, but I do hope to see you at some assembly, and herewith request the honour of a dance with each of you."

Lady Rowland, beginning to thaw, smiled and said, "I do not dance, sir. But I see no objection to your soliciting my daughters, should we happen to be present at the same assembly."

"I shall make it a point to be present at every possible party to which I am invited, in the hopes of seeing you," he said, a twinkle in his dark eyes taking the fulsomeness from his compliment.

Georgie said shrewdly, "We hope your opportunity will come at Almack's."

As she expected, his face fell, for Almack's was generally considered by all smart young bucks, and especially the Corinthian set to which Mr. Dandridge evidently belonged, as the most dull, flat, and insipid way to spend an evening. But Mr. Dandridge was made of sterner stuff, and he recovered swiftly. With an amused smile at Georgie, he said, "I am such a sad rattle that I doubt the Patronesses will allow me in the door, but I will most certainly make the attempt. Please, do not let me keep you out here in the cold for another moment." He stepped aside and ushered them through the welcomingly open door of the inn.

In the private parlour--this one unmarred by any sign of Lady Shipton--Cecilia at once ran to the window to watch Mr. Dandridge's departure. "He is slap up to the echo, is he not?"

Lady Rowland snapped, "Cecilia, where on earth did you learn that term? Never use it again."

"No, Mama," Cecilia replied, in that tone Georgie knew meant she intended to do so, but not again within her mother's hearing. "I mean, he seems very fine and gentlemanly."

Lady Rowland stripped off her gloves and raised her hands to untie her bonnet. "I must say, I found him much more genteel than I expected. He had a reputation as a great rake before he went to the Continent, but I daresay that being an officer has matured him. His manners are more familiar than I like, but not objectionable."

"Then we can dance with him, if he asks us?"

"You may. And I am sure he will ask you, for he will have to go very far to find two more lovely girls."

Georgie, busy with her own bonnet, was grateful her mother could not see her expression. While she objected to compliments no more than any other young woman did, she worried about Cecilia. Already the belle of Henniston and every other village for miles around Rowland Hall, Cecilia was well on her way to being not only vain, but a dreadful flirt, and was both determined and positive that her first Season would be even more successful than Georgie's had been. In vain had Georgie explained to her that a good part of her popularity was due, not to her looks, charm, and grace, but to the fact that she was one of the Miss Rowlands of Rowland Hall, and also that in their restricted society, where they dined with barely twenty families, Cecilia shone in a way that she would fail to do in London, where she would be only one of many beauties, some of them diamonds of the first water.

She refrained from speaking now, however, because her previous attempts to curb her mother's praise had all gone for nothing. Lady Rowland thought it important and needful to compliment her daughters. Georgie might have considered it in the same light, if her mother had found something admirable about them beyond their good looks and accomplishments in music and drawing.

# *Chapter 9*

Sir Henry Becknall, like his elder sister, had inherited a tidy sum of money. Unlike her, his wants were simple. He had a house in town because being in town was necessary for him, and he had a large house because peace and quiet were even more essential to him. Other than this elegant home on Grosvenor Street, however, he purchased little for himself and invested his funds with canny wisdom. The result was that the annual visit of his sister, even with the necessity of holding a ball and several parties for his nieces, was little trouble to him, the chief drawback being that it made peace and quiet difficult and sometimes impossible to achieve. Luckily for Lady Rowland, he had a great fondness for Georgiana, in whom he saw some reflection of himself, and he also had a sense of family duty, which made him unable to deny his sister any reasonable request when she had been widowed.

The disturbance of a number of women in his household was made more acceptable to him by his declaring his office, a large room on the ground floor, adjacent to the library, as strictly off limits to anyone. In this room he pursued his true avocation--he wrote books. His books were chiefly histories, with forays into the analysis of social and economic influence not only in

England but also in those nations which had ties to England, both good and bad, including those in Europe and Asia, and also including that ex-colony now called America. These books were not only well-written, insightful, and erudite, but useful enough to have earned for him a knighthood.

He was in his office, surrounded by piles of reference books and wrestling with a particularly involved bit of prose, when a discreet knock on the door brought his head up. His glasses slipped down his nose, and he absently removed and polished them with a handkerchief as he said, "What? What is it, Addison? Oh, come in, come in."

His butler opened the door with awful dignity. "Lady Rowland, Miss Rowland, and Miss Cecilia have this moment arrived, sir," he said lugubriously. At threescore and three years, Addison was more than twenty years older than Sir Henry, but age was not why he spoke now in a wavering voice, with a pronounced stoop to his shoulders. He did these things as a subtle protest against this annual invasion, and he'd been doing it since Lady Rowland's first visit, two years after Rowland himself had died and she had given up their town house to their son and heir. This protest was, perhaps, too subtle, for as always Sir Henry failed to see the danger signs of encroaching collapse from old age and overwork, and said only, "Let Mrs. Haycock settle them, Addison. Come and fetch me when they have been served refreshment."

"Yes, sir," Addison said gloomily, and if he shut the door a trifle loudly, Sir Henry, already absorbed once more in his passage, did not notice.

Sir Henry bore all the mien of a scholar lost in his books, absentminded to the point of living in a fog, his pale blue eyes regarding the world as an interesting study rather than a place in which he actually lived. However, he was, in fact, quite shrewd. He knew how his sister was after a journey of any length, and he trusted Addison and his housekeeper to attend to Lady Rowland before he would have to speak with her. They would see to it that her bags were conveyed to her usual room and unpacked exactly as she wished, and that her pelisse and bonnet were gently removed and discreetly whisked away. They would make her comfortable in the South Drawing Room with a cheerful fire and screens placed to best prevent drafts, and provide her with an excellent tea. Therefore, by the time he was summoned by Addison once more, his sister would have already poured out her complaints about her journey and would be consuming cakes which would, he trusted, slow down her powers of speech to a tolerable point.

He rose on Addison's entry and allowed the butler to help him into his waistcoat and coat, which, although of good cut and quality cloth, were not so tight as to require the offices of his valet to get him into them. Indeed, Crowley, his valet, truly had little to do. Although fastidiously neat, Sir Henry had no desire to cut a fashionable figure. Of average height and physique, he allowed no aids to the presentation of his form, such as buckram wadding in the shoulders of his coats or sand to fill out the calves of his stockings. His fair hair, as thick and lustrous as his sister's, was left to fall as it would with a quick brushing, since he had not the patience to have it curled and artfully arranged. And such adjuncts to a gentleman's person that were considered proper, such as fobs and seals, he found interfered with his work and dispensed with completely.

The only reason that Crowley had not moved on to a more satisfactory master was that he had formerly served Sir Henry's father, and a combination of age, familiarity with the household, and family loyalty prevented him not only from deserting his post for a better, but also from uttering a word of complaint. Like Addison, his protests were subtle, voiced mostly in heavy sighs, and Sir Henry ignored those as easily as he did Addison's apparent declines.

Telling Addison to please not neglect to bring him some brandy, he mounted the wide stair to the second floor and ventured into his drawing room. He found a charming scene there. His sister, devouring cakes in a way that often made him wonder how she maintained her figure, was before the fire, dressed as always in the height of fashion, her gown a colourful flower blooming in the muted shades with which the room was decorated. On the couch were his two nieces, their arms about each other's waists, their heads bent over some feminine magazine, Georgiana's dusky curls and Cecilia's divinely fair ones mingling with delightful harmony. When he entered, both looked up, and Georgie, with whom he had always been first oars, bounded to her feet and came to him, to hug him and give him a kiss on the cheek with a familiarity that made her mother cluck disparagingly, but which made Sir Henry glow with pleasure.

"Uncle Henry! You see we have descended on you again."

"And I am glad to see you."

"Gammon. You'd love to see us all with Charles, no matter how sweet you are to protest to the contrary. But we shall make every endeavor not to cut up your peace," she promised.

"*You* never do cut up my peace," he retorted. For a moment, they smiled at each other with complete understanding. Then he turned to his sister, asked how her journey had gone, and sat down prepared to at least look attentive. Lady Rowland's cascade of troubles was enlivened, this time, by the mention of Lady Shipton. "I could not give her the cut direct, not with her being so obliging, but I did not speak to her any more than was absolutely required," she informed him.

"Quite proper," he murmured in his absent way, knowing she required no more for the conversation than the assurance that he was still awake.

When Lady Rowland had finished describing the rigors of their journey, discussed a ball for Cecilia's introduction to society at some length, and regretted that Cecilia could not be presented at Court, to all of which Sir Henry continued to respond with nods and murmurs in the appropriate places, she declared that they were all exhausted and would retire immediately after supper. But in this she was mistaken. She and Cecilia did go upstairs, but Georgie remained behind, joining her uncle in his enormous Library. "Do you mind terribly, Uncle Henry? Should I go away?" she asked prettily.

He set aside his book, removed his glasses, and gestured to the chair nearest him. "You know I am always happy to talk to you."

She curled up in the chair in a way that would have given her mother a spasm, and asked what he was reading. For a while they spoke of books, and then she recollected loaning his latest to Richard, and of Richard's astonishing way of trying to amuse and divert her. "I want you to know I received another proposal of marriage," she told him.

"Did you? How delightful. I take it, since your mother did not mention it, that you not only rejected the fellow, but that you neglected to mention it to her?"

Georgie laughed. "You will never guess who it was. Richard!"

Sir Henry said mildly, "He has shown some attachment to you..."

But Georgie interrupted him with another gurgle of laughter. "It was all in jest. He caught me at a time when I was nearly overwhelmed and quite frustrated, and he promised to marry me and take me away from it all. He succeeded in his object, because he made me laugh, and as he knows better than anyone, I always feel much more able to deal with everything after a good laugh."

"A dangerous joke," Sir Henry smiled. "What would he have done if you had accepted him?"

That idea had not before occurred to her, and it increased her merriment. "I should have done so, just to have seen the look of horror on his face! What a wasted opportunity."

"Well, in your defence, you did say you were overwhelmed."

"We must give Richard full credit for such admirable courage and selflessness, in taking such a chance just to divert me," she laughed.

"Indeed, I know he has long been a good friend to all of you, but that is going beyond the call of duty. My dear, you are sure he was not serious?"

She found this amusing, too. "Uncle Henry! How could that be possible? Richard? Who loves a good joke more than food or wine? Indeed, if I had accepted him, he most likely would have had some creditable tale up his sleeve to deny it all."

"Perhaps insanity. For what is love but insanity?" Sir Henry mused.

She tilted her head to gaze at him fondly. "I do so miss you when I am in the country. You say the drollest things, you never are shocked at what I say, and you never have to ask, *What do you mean?*"

"I can say the same of you. Speaking of insanity, is this coming-out like to run you mad?"

"Probably. But I shall have you here to pull me back from the brink."

She sobered and quieted, toying with the fringe on the edge of her shawl. Knowing these symptoms, Sir Henry folded his hands and said, "Come, come. Out with it, my girl. What did you really wish to speak to me about?"

She bit her lip. "Lady Shipton, sir."

"Ah."

"Do you know her?"

"I have never met her, but naturally I have heard of her."

"Well, I have not. She was so kind to us, so ladylike. Mother treated her as though she was... I do not know what. But I liked her. Or I think I *could* like her, if I had the chance. I felt so badly to have to stand by and see her so rudely snubbed. Will you tell me why my mother feels she is so unfit for us to know? To even acknowledge with anything more than a nod in passing?"

"I can, I think. But your mother would not approve of me doing so. She would not consider it fit for your young ears."

"Uncle Henry," she protested, "I have read the Greeks. What could possibly shock me?"

Sir Henry's eyes twinkled. "If your mother knew that, we would both be in the suds. Very well, I will tell you. Lady Shipton, before her marriage into the peerage, was an actress."

Georgie sat upright. "An Opera dancer?"

He frowned. "Who told you about those?"

"Richard, of course. Was she?"

"No. She was a serious actress, but still, an actress and from an unknown but very likely common background. She was also somewhat less than respectable in her personal life," he hedged.

"Let's have the tree with no bark on it. Was she a courtesan?"

He looked pained. "I hope you do not use those terms anywhere but in this room. Not precisely a courtesan, for her reputation was that she was faithful to whatever man happened to be keeping her at the time. Shipton, who was some thirty years her senior, was completely besotted with her. I remember my father laughing about it, especially when he made their relationship regular by proposing marriage to her."

Georgie was wide-eyed. "It is very hard to believe all this about the lady I met."

"As I understand it, she was a devoted and faithful wife to Shipton. Certainly he was a most happy man right up to the day that he died. And I have not heard that she has taken a lover since. I imagine that security and a social status were her goals, and to a degree she has achieved them. She is reputed to be a great beauty. Is she?"

"Indeed she is. One of the most beautiful women I have ever seen, and exceedingly elegant."

"Then I doubt a mere passing acquaintance with her will do you harm."

"I think it is terribly unfair. She could not help but be born in her own status, but she made the best of it, and if she has led a blameless life since her marriage, why should she be so scorned?"

"Lay down your cudgels, Georgie. She does not need your defence, spirited and good-hearted as it is. Her blameless life since marrying, and Lord Shipton's influence, have gained her entry into the homes of all but the highest sticklers. Of course, Shipton having left her a good ten thousand a year did not harm her standing."

"You paint the picture of a calculating woman, Uncle Henry, but that is not the impression I received. I thought her kind."

"Then I sincerely hope you are right. The world wants kindness, and to discover it in the scandalous must be a good sign for all of humanity."

# Chapter 10

Lady Rowland was laid upon her bed all the following day, prostrate with fatigue, by which was meant that she drifted to the couch in her sitting room and remained there, swathed in shawls, an elegantly interesting object of compassion for her dresser Bridges, and as much trouble as possible for Mrs. Haycock and the maids. Her daughters, being made of sterner stuff, consumed a substantial breakfast and then set out to view the shops and millineries, with an eye to determining how best and most quickly to fit out Cecilia in a way that satisfied both that young lady and their mother.

Cecilia was looking her best, her natural charms enhanced by the heightened colour and sparkling eyes given her by her excitement. She had been in London before, but always as a schoolgirl, in the company of Puddles, and never on Bond Street or any other fashionable walk. Not only was she with her sister on this occasion, but she was conscious of looking her best in her walking dress of figured muslin with its demure double flounce and a dark blue, subtly striped pelisse edged with tiny knots of silver thread.

Added to the exhilaration of being set free of the chaperonage of Miss Puddleforth and wearing her most fashionable walking dress, she was conscious of a kind of inner awareness that this was *her* Season. No more would she be sitting home while Georgie and her mother went out at night, or be forced to listen with complaisance to Lady Rowland's account of Georgie's triumphs. This time, *she* would be the one to be having triumphs. Yes, and making conquests, too. She had every intention of bettering her sister by ending this Season with a betrothal. She gazed around them at the smart, fashionable people as much as, or perhaps even more than, she gazed into shop windows, viewing each lady as a person to be emulated or not, and viewing each gentleman as a possible marriage partner, or not.

They stopped before a milliners' window for Georgie to point out to her a fetching bonnet, trimmed with rucked silk ribbon. But Cecilia was more captivated by the hat that was next to it, a charming confection with a high crown and a narrow perky brim, covered with gauze, and trimmed with a single, perfectly curled ostrich feather dyed to match. "Is that not the most delightful hat you have ever seen?" she exclaimed.

Georgie agreed. "But it is entirely unsuitable for a girl in her first Season, or, indeed, any unmarried girl."

"That is too bad. It seems ridiculous that, simply because a girl is just now come out, she must be restricted to the most insipid colours and sober gowns."

"I believe the custom is intended to make the married state more desirable for us," Georgie said sagely.

But Cecilia had not lived with Georgie all her life to miss the twinkle in the eye that accompanied this. She laughed and took her sister's arm. Before they turned away, she caught a clear glimpse of her reflection, and although she largely approved of what she saw, she realized that, in one point, she was lacking. The way her fair hair was neatly braided upon her crown suddenly looked dowdy and childlike, and she cried, "I must get my hair cut!"

"You must and you shall. Puddles will cut it for you tonight. So while you are observing all the world going by, try to decide how you would like to have it cropped and curled. And also allow me to point out to you that we are too early for most of the fashionable crowd to be about, so you should save your observing for later." She sighed. "I would love to take you for a drive in the Park this afternoon, but I doubt that Richard has yet arrived with our horses and carriage."

Despite the early hour, they paused to greet many acquaintances of Georgie's. She was a popular girl. To a naturally sunny nature and good manners, she added the kind of attentiveness that prompted her to introduce her own dance partners to girls who might otherwise have been left standing, and she never spent her entire time at a party voting it a sad crush and affecting a sophisticated boredom.

With the idea of balls, Venetian breakfasts, musical evenings, al fresco outings, and other assemblies very much in the forefront of her mind, Cecilia paid close attention to her sister's advice at all times. When Georgie murmured, "Here comes Lady Althrop, dreadful dragon, two spotty sons, but a friend of the Countess Lieven," or "Mrs. Wellaby and her daughter, first style of elegance, you'd do worse than to copy them," Cecilia listened and learned. Still, she could not but feel somewhat envious. Therefore, when she saw an acquaintance who did not have to be introduced to her by Georgie, her spirits were buoyant.

When this person approached her, she and Georgie had come to a dress shop, and Georgie had gone in to inquire about a gown she was sure their mother would want for herself. Uninterested in anything her mother might acquire, Cecilia remained outside beside the step, indulging herself with watching the increasing numbers of passers-by, and hence was happily alone when Mr. Dandridge strolled toward her. She was not so vulgar as to wave or call out, or in any other way to draw attention to herself, but as he drew near, Mr. Dandridge obviously recognized her and was equally obviously as pleased to see her as she was to see him. He swept off his hat with a graceful bow. "Miss Cecilia Rowland," he said, gratifying her by having recollected her name and by the pleasure in his voice when he said it. "I see you have arrived, despite all the possible mishaps along that tedious road that might have delayed you further."

She started to giggle at his teasing tone, but turned it to a smile. Mr. Dandridge noticed and said, "No, do not spoil it. Go ahead and laugh."

"I do not think I shall. Mama says that giggling makes a girl look like a country bumpkin, and I do not want to be mistaken for such."

"No one who sees you would mistake you for any kind of a bumpkin, country or otherwise. You are entirely safe to delight us with your laughter. But I am going to frown on you now, I think. Where, Miss Rowland, is your chaperone? Surely you are not alone."

"My sister is with me."

He looked around. "Do you know, I thought I had a tolerable memory of her face, but I do not recognize her anywhere about. Point her out to me, so that I do not appear rude by ignoring her in my ignorance."

This time she did laugh, a little gurgle which, though quickly stifled, made him smile back at her. "She is inside this store, sir, as I am sure you have guessed."

"You have found me out. How are you enjoying your first day in London?"

"Prodigiously. But it is not my first day in London, sir. I have come here the past three years with my sister."

"Not possible. I would have met you."

"I was a schoolgirl. You would not have noticed me."

"I beg to differ, but I shall hold my compliments for later. I am sure you are about the business of tricking yourself out in the finest togs, and any compliment I give you now would have to be bettered when next I see you, in which case I shall overreach myself and sound like a coxcomb. Will you visit the sights while you are here? Astley's, perhaps, and the Royal Menagerie?"

"I have seen all those, sir. Puddles--Miss Puddleforth, my governess-- took me to all of them. I am, however, eagerly looking forward to those sights with which I have not yet become familiar, such as the opera and the theatre."

"So you will cut your hair and add culture to your life."

"In a word, sir, yes."

"An excellent plan." Smiling down at her, he said, "I am going to leave you now, if reluctantly."

"You have another engagement?"

"Not at all. I am completely at leisure. But as I am sure your sister and mother have mentioned to you--or at least I hope they have, or they shan't be doing their duty!--I have a reputation for being a dangerous rake. It was earned in my youth, I assure you, but even so, it will not add to your consequence to be seen talking to me in so public a place as this, with no chaperone about." The smile in his eyes invited her to see the humour of his situation, but he was serious, for he made his bow with a polite goodbye and a hope that he would see her again soon, and in better circumstances.

Georgie emerged just as he left, and frowned. "Were you just talking to Mr. Dandridge?"

Her tone put Cecilia's back up. "We were just passing the time of day," she said stiffly.

"It is not a good idea for you to--"

"Oh, I know. He said so himself, so would speak to me for no more than a moment, out of common courtesy."

"That's more delicacy than I'd expect from a man of his reputation." She glanced at her sister's sparkling eyes and said, "Flirt with him if you will, Cecy, but no more than that. He is not a proper man for you to know."

"I like him. He reminds me of Richard."

"If you cannot see the difference between Richard and that man, then you need my guidance more than I realized."

She was joking, and laughed, but Cecilia's resentment did not fade. She simply ignored it, laughed as well, and linked her arm with Georgie's to go on their way.

# Chapter 11

Since guarding her sister from rakes and fortune-hunters was one of the primary duties Georgie had assumed when she'd agreed to help bring Cecilia out, seeing her sister willing to encourage the attentions of Mr. Dandridge troubled Georgie's peace of mind, something she mentioned later that day to Mr. Harding. She did not, however, mention it to her mother, nor was she so foolish as to bring it up again to Cecilia. She recognized that stubborn look on Cecy's face, and knew that her hands on the reins would have to be light, and that Cecy would respond much better to distraction than to a lecture.

Therefore, when they arrived home and found their mother much revived, she had the happy thought of asking about what warehouses they should do best to try. In minutes, Cecilia and Lady Rowland had their heads together, wholly absorbed in deciding on the virtues of various muslins, twills, silks, and sarcenets, and discussing at length what trims, buttons, ribbons, feathers, jewelry, boots, reticules, and other appendages to female apparel would be needed. Mr. Dandridge was forgotten. Georgie, working on her embroidery, was content that this discussion would keep them occupied for some time, the styles of bonnets alone being enough for a good half hour, and therefore she would have leisure to ponder what to do about him.

She was not much of a needlewoman and quickly tired both of this occupation and of the thought of Mr. Dandridge, but before she risked drawing attention to herself by rising to get a book, and thereby being pulled into the conversation, she got a welcome diversion in the form of Mr. Harding.

He followed hard on the heels of Addison's announcing him, sure of his welcome. He stopped just inside the room, stared at the stack of magazines and fabric samples, and, with that informality that Lady Rowland so deprecated, said, "Good God. I seem to have arrived at a most inopportune moment."

Unable to resist teasing him, Georgie put aside her hoop and said, "On the contrary, we need a male opinion. Do not you agree, Mama?"

Lady Rowland said snubbingly, "How do you do, Mr. Harding. So nice to see you. Shall I have Addison bring you some refreshment?"

"No, I thank you, ma'am. I drove myself over and do not wish to keep my horses standing. I am very sure that you do not need a male opinion," this to Georgie, "since the conversation seems to be, by all indications, completely devoted to fashion."

"But we must know whether a gentleman would prefer, let us say for example, a sprigged or a figured muslin on a lady he might take walking."

"The greater part of my sex--indeed, probably all of us--would scarcely know the difference between one gown and the next, and would doubtless not even notice what you wore at all, unless it were uncommonly inappropriate or garish. If Cecilia, for example, were to wear a crimson opera cloak over a pomona green evening dress while receiving morning visitors here in this drawing room, I might notice it, but I doubt it would do more to my mind than to make me wonder why she did so."

Georgie laughed. "I can never put you out of countenance."

"*That*, I assure you, is not the case."

"I wish that were so. But your horses await you. Tell us the purpose of your call. Is it to tell me our own horses are arrived safely?"

"You have hit it in one. Not that it was difficult for a girl of your understanding, since, having no inclination to be scolded, I would never have dared to call until they were arrived. Bloomsbury brought them on the last stage this morning, and they are now resting, eating their heads off, and in fine fettle."

Lady Rowland beamed on him. "That is so kind of you, Mr. Harding. And such good news. Truly, I do not know what we should do without your kindness."

"Let Charles keep them for us," Georgie said at once.

"But Charles is so far away! It would be so inconvenient for the footmen and take so much more time!"

"Whereas I," said Mr. Harding, "am so conveniently situated."

"And so kind," Lady Rowland added, resolutely ignoring the edge of sarcasm in his voice. "Can you please tell Bloomsbury that we shall require the landaulet tomorrow? As early as can be arranged after one."

Mr. Harding bowed an assent. "Now, I must go, but before I do, I have brought my curricle. Would either of you young ladies care to drive in the Park? It is close to the fashionable hour, after all."

Cecilia said, "You mean Georgie by this invitation, I am positive. It would not entertain you at all to take me up with you."

"I am not so sure. The fact that you have only just turned eighteen and are therefore, like most young girls, silly beyond comprehension, must be weighed against the entertainment that will be provided by all your suitors staring daggers at me and doing ridiculous things to get your attention."

Not at all disliking this oddly phrased compliment, Cecilia laughed. "But I have only been in town for a day, Mr. Harding. I have no suitors."

"Then I must definitely request Georgiana as my companion. I am sure she must have a few here in town, even this early in the Season."

Georgie, who could think of nothing she would like better than to be in an open carriage on a sunny day, ran off to get her hat and pelisse, and in moments, Mr. Harding was handing her into the curricle. He dismissed his groom and guided his pair expertly into the street. After admiring his style for a moment, aloud, Georgie said, "You know, it is not entirely true that Cecilia has no suitors yet."

"Oh, come! Who could she have possibly met in less than four and twenty hours?"

"We actually met him on the road here. He introduced himself to us, but why, I do not know."

"Perhaps because he has eyes enough to see two very pretty girls, but not manners or patience enough to wait for a proper introduction. That seems simple enough. But you seem to be weaving something sinister from it."

"Not sinister! But worrisome. It is Mr. Neil Dandridge."

"Ah. That explains it all."

"Mama does not agree. She thinks him charming. And while she has warned Cecy not to take him seriously, I cannot but think that he could pose a danger to her." She turned her face up to his. "What do you think? Am I being missish about this?"

"You have never been missish in your life. Well, perhaps once, in the case of that very large beetle..."

"Richard! Do stop throwing things up to me that happened when I was a child!"

He grinned. "Avoiding that topic, and dismissing that instance, I have generally found you to be a girl of good sense."

"And in this instance?"

He frowned, delaying his answer until he'd navigated them safely into the Park and was proceeding along at a correct trot. "I am not personally acquainted with Dandridge or any of his set, but I have heard rumors. All the world knows he must marry money, and while I would not say that Cecilia's portion is such that would tempt a fortune hunter, one can never be sure, or too careful. His reputation is not that of a libertine, so I doubt her virtue is at stake, but her heart may well be. He is supposedly dangerous to females with susceptible hearts, and Cecilia's is so. He is a Corinthian of some note; Winborne knows his crowd; I shall ask him about it tonight."

"Thank you, Richard." She smiled. "This is the second time in two days that I have asked a friend about someone, and gotten rumors for an answer."

"Our society is conversationally incestuous; we only talk about each other. Who was this other friend, and what were the rumors that he or she gave you?"

"I speak of Uncle Henry. I was asking him about Lady Shipton, whom we also met on the road."

His brows went up, and he smiled. "Which might be an explanation as to why Dandridge was from town. Sits the wind in that quarter, does it?"

"What do you mean?"

"The widow Lady Shipton was left very well off. I imagine Dandridge is now pursuing her. He will catch cold at that, however. She is far too canny."

"You know her?"

"Yes, I do. She often holds parties of a more intellectual sort than what is commonly given during the Season, and is quite a patroness of the arts."

"Do you like her?"

"Why does that matter?" he asked, amused.

"Oh, Richard, do not tease. You do, do you not?"

"I will confess it. The lady has charm and beauty, but most of all, she has a mind which she actually uses, and on a regular basis, too."

"You know, part of my delight in your company is that you are one of the few men I have met who not only desires an independent mind in a woman, but requires it."

"What a comment on my sex. Accurate, but unkind."

"But about Lady Shipton...her past does not bother you?"

"Sir Henry told you about that? The man has no restraint." Stopping her before she could protest again, he said, "I will answer you, so pray do not jump up and down in that hoydenish way. No, her past does not trouble me. Can you think of a single reason why it should? She has left all that behind and become so respectable that she would be boring, if her nature were not so lively and amusing. Now, why do you look so smug?"

"Because I liked her very much, but Mama refuses to give her more than a nod. I do wish I could further the acquaintance. But that is hopeless, as long as I am in Mama's house."

"As far as that goes, you are in your Uncle Henry's house. But otherwise, I see your problem. It is a pity, you know, that you did not accept my proposal while you had the chance. We could get married at once, and I would escort you to one of Lady Shipton's parties, which you would enjoy immensely."

"Would you really?" Georgie asked, regretting, as Cecilia had, and not for the first time, the differences in custom that prevailed between the license allowed a married woman and that *not* allowed to a single girl.

"I would. I think you would enjoy yourself. And, to add to the benefit, you could be buying your wedding clothes now, instead of worrying about white and pastel muslins for Cecilia. Are you sure you will not change your mind?"

"You would be well served if I said yes, you know. Then you would be in a fix."

"A dreadful one." He gave an exaggerated sigh. "Even the promise of these treats will not bribe you into marriage, I take it?"

"It will take a great deal more than that." She burst into laughter and hugged his arm. "You are so good for me."

"I am, for it takes much to amuse you at times."

"I am sorry to be such trouble," she said sincerely.

He smiled down at her. "Is it the part of a friend to complain, or apologize, for being of use to one another?"

# Chapter 12

Cecilia's come-out ball was one of the first of the Season, since all three women were desirous of launching Cecilia into the ton at the earliest opportunity. London was thin of company still, but much of the fashionable world turned out between ten and midnight, and yet more shortly after, making it their second party of the evening. The success was partly due to Lady Rowland's wide acquaintance and Georgie's tireless efforts at leaving her card and paying morning visits with Cecilia, and partly to Sir Henry's patronage. Sir Henry rarely entertained, but when he did, it was well known that he spared no expense, and that his ballroom was of just the size to be certain that the affair would be called a sad crush without it being so crowded that one could not move through it. The music was provided by a band of quality; the refreshments were superior in both flavor and presentation; and there was never a lack of champagne, sherry, and wine.

Among those asked to the dinner beforehand was Lady Jersey, and Georgie considered herself fortunate that this capriciously haughty patroness of Almack's accepted the invitation. Not only did Lady Jersey promise the much-desired vouchers to Almack's, but she had taken one of her unaccountable fancies to Mr. Harding. Although Lady Rowland would not have failed to include such an old family friend and benefactor as Mr. Harding in the invitations, her nervousness about what he might say to offend this person or that were abated to a degree by Lady Jersey's pleasure in his company.

Georgie, in fact, barely got the chance to talk to him at all until they danced during the ball, and by then she was in high flight, for Cecilia was a definite success. She had been pronounced by Lady Jersey a prettily behaved girl and not at all insipid, so Lady Rowland was in alt.

Cecilia was looking her very best in a yellow satin gown with a three-quarter overdress of figured crepe, fastened with tiny silk rosebuds, and bearing a corsage of yellow roses which had been a gift from Mr. Harding, who had been informed of the colour of her gown. Her newly cropped hair was bound up with a yellow silk ribbon and one of Mr. Harding's roses, and for jewelry she wore, quite properly, nothing more than a simple necklace of pearls.

Circulating through the room, Georgie was gratified to hear praise on all sides for Cecilia's beauty, manners, and simplicity of dress. While Lady Rowland accepted all the glory for this, Georgie had even greater pleasure in hearing it, since her pleasure was unalloyed by any vanity or apprehension.

She was also greatly gratified, if unsurprised, that Cecilia never once lacked for a partner in the dancing. Naturally she was led out first by Sir Henry, who, as he had for Georgiana, overcame his dislike of a crush with his sense of family duty and his affection for his nieces. After that, Mr. Harding led her out, and to Georgie's pleasure, once their set was finished, he led her, not back to her mother, but to young Lord Erringfield, to whom he introduced her. Erringfield was known to be something of a connoisseur of young ladies, and his dancing with Cecilia and his evident enjoyment of the half hour he spent in her company made certain that she was so in demand that she was obliged to regretfully turn some gentlemen away.

With nothing more to concern her, Georgie accepted Mr. Harding's hand for a set, but her conversation was so much of Cecilia that he protested as they went down the row, "Honestly, you must not think I am not ecstatic for you, as I am. In fact, I am willing and even happy to celebrate any of your triumphs. But not for half an hour altogether!"

"Abominable man. You should at least pretend to find delightful any subject a lady cares to discuss during your dance with her."

"Perhaps you are right. But this is something with which I have no previous experience."

"No previous experience with conversation while dancing! Richard, you are absurd!"

"I meant that I have never before in all of my life danced with a woman whose entire discourse was about *another woman.*"

She laughed at this, and when the dance brought them back together, she promised him to converse no more on Cecilia. She kept her word, although she was sorely tempted when Mr. Harding took her down to supper and their party was joined by Erringfield, escorting Cecilia and evidently quite happy in his choice.

Her mood was not so pleased when next she stood up with Mr. Harding. However, when he asked her what made her frown so, she did her best to continue to honour her vow and said she could not tell him for that reason.

"Do not be silly, Georgie," he said trenchantly. "I cannot wish to be addled with talk of gowns and hair and flowers and beaux, but if there is something which vexes you, naturally I am willing to lend an ear. Is it something with which I can help?"

Georgie lowered her voice so that only he could hear. "It is that Cecilia is now dancing with Mr. Dandridge."

"I admit to being surprised he was invited," Mr. Harding observed, likewise discreetly lowering his voice.

"Mama would invite him, despite my protest. She said he would add consequence to the ball. What she meant is that she believes we could not have too many eligible young men attend."

"I am sure she never would say anything so vulgar," he said. "What she was thinking, however, we shall leave to our imaginations, and I will not dispute you on that point."

"Indeed you will not, since you know us all far too well, even Mama. I suppose I must be glad he came so late and cannot be particular in his attention to her. Although," she went on with her usual optimism, "perhaps I am mistaken, drawn by my own partiality to believe him more entranced by Cecilia than he is."

She fell silent, and Mr. Harding observed, "You frown again. People will think I am not entertaining you. You do me great injustice, for being entertaining is one of my few known virtues. What is it now, you tiresome girl?"

She smiled at this, but spoke soberly. "I am thinking that I should be less concerned about his attention to her, and more concerned about her attention to *him*. For she seems to be enjoying herself more in his company than in any other."

"Take heart that she is appearing to excellent advantage, since her pleasure improves her looks immensely. There are at least ten gentlemen who, being denied her hand in the dance, have slighted every other woman in the room and are now leaning picturesquely against the wall, glowering at Dandridge. In fact, I doubt you shall have to concern yourself about him at all. By this time next week, one of those ten at least will have called him out, and he will either be dead, or have killed his man and be forced to leave the country."

"Or be wounded and an object of even greater interest! I see your purpose. You exaggerate my feelings in order to make them appear as trivial as they are. I hope you are right."

"Even if I were not, every girl must break her heart at some point. You did, after all, over that fellow in a red coat, and it did you no lasting harm."

"Capt. Trevor! I had all but forgotten him. A schoolgirl's infatuation, and you are unkind to bring it up."

"Infatuation? When you wept and were indisposed for company for two days together? We all feared for your health, I assure you."

"You are right, however teasingly you phrase it. I did indeed think my heart was broken when he left the area without so much as an adieu to me, yet it did me no harm. In fact, in the long run, it did me much good."

"Then why would you deny Cecilia the benefit of suffering for unrequited love?"

She sobered. "I know it to be foolish, but I'd prevent her from suffering for anything."

"Thereby ruining her character. She is not a child any longer. You must let her grow by experience, for no one, man or woman, ever yet matured by precept."

"You are right yet again. In fact, it is lowering to me to realize that I take greater care for her now than I did when she actually *was* a child."

"That is because you are guarding her heart now, not worrying about her scraping her knee or tearing her gown."

Her smile was warm and grateful. "I do not know how you manage it, but you always seem to know exactly what to say. You have eased my worry and at the same time set me up again in my own conceit."

"Then let me add this, and we shall cease talking about the chit and discuss something of sense. Although the ten Byronically brooding gentlemen I mentioned were, as you surmised, completely from my imagination, I still believe that Cecilia shall be so besieged with suitors that Neil Dandridge will be lost among them."

# Chapter 13

The next day seemed to prove Mr. Harding's sanguine prediction. Mr. Dandridge's gift of an elegant posy was but one of many, and not even the best of them, and Cecilia showed no disposition to treasure it above any of the rest. She was rather uniform in her pleasure and charming in her delighted surprise at the number of visitors they received throughout that day and the next, and although Lady Rowland complained, "Is the knocker never still?", she was as thrilled as were her daughters.

Even better, cards of invitation began to pour in. Although Georgie had known it would be so, even she was elated when she saw that they would be engaged for three different parties in the same night. Cecilia's success was assured. Mothers with eligible sons hastened to arrange events in which the Rowland girls could be included, and other hostesses, already Lady Rowland's friends and Georgiana's admirers, and charmed by Cecilia's unassuming, pleasant manners, were happy to add them to their invitations. Only those mothers with unusually plain unmarried daughters chose to ignore them.

However, as two weeks of an endless round of pleasures blissfully passed, it became apparent to Georgie that, despite all her attempts to introduce Cecilia to every possible young man who might take her fancy, and despite the fact that Cecilia was far too well-bred to expose herself in any way to gossip or speculation, her partiality had settled on Mr. Dandridge above all others. Georgie's sole venture into discussing the subject, however, was not taken well. She tried to be subtle, introducing Mr. Dandridge's name while discussing others one day, as she and Cecilia were putting on their bonnets, about to pay a call. She said simply, "And of course Mr. Dandridge is most charming as well. Such a pity he is so ineligible."

"Ineligible?" Cecilia said. "Why should he be considered so?"

Since her tone was mild, Georgie ventured to explain. "Apart from his reputation, he is a known gamester, is addicted to every kind of sport, and has not a feather to fly with."

Cecilia turned to her and said, "To be addicted to sport is infinitely preferable, to my way of thinking, than to be a dandy. And to marry only for the sake of money seems to me abhorrent."

"If you did not have it, you would not say so. Those who are not comfortably settled already must find some way to become so, and marrying well is by far the easiest and most socially acceptable means of accomplishing it."

Cecilia's little chin lifted. "Then I consider myself most fortunate, not to be forced to be mercenary in my likings, and I pity those who are not as happily circumstanced as I."

"This does your heart credit, but do please keep it in mind when you listen to Mr. Dandridge's compliments."

"I will, if you insist, and also to those of many others. Are you not ready yet? We should go."

This unsatisfactory conversation had an even more unsatisfactory result, for at the Coxe's ball that evening, in what Georgie was certain was a direct rebellion against her hint, rather than paying less attention to Mr. Dandridge, Cecilia instead paid him even more. Mr. Harding, who appeared at Georgie's elbow while she was regarding their laughing conversation with displeasure, said, "You made the mistake of trying to hint her away?"

"I did, and I am still lashing myself about it, so do not you add to my mortification."

"I would not dream of it. Shall I go separate them?"

"You are very kind to think of that, but she will believe I sent you."

"Which would only make things worse," he agreed. "Do you want me to send Winborne? That may be more subtle, and he will not resent the charge. In fact, he is quite taken with her."

"I gathered that when he showed such pleasure at joining the three of us in the landaulet yesterday. But Cecilia is not a simpleton." Then, her attention was distracted by the sight of someone she knew and had not expected to see. Not ten feet away, Lady Shipton was just separating herself from a conversation with their hostess. Georgie felt again the pangs of envy at the lady's beauty and elegance. She wore a gown of emerald silk in the very latest fashion, which had undoubtedly cost as much as all of Georgie's own gowns combined. A tasteful, matching set of diamonds adorned her slender throat, her ears, and her flaming hair. Her walk and her air were both graceful and compelling, yet did not call attention to themselves, and Georgie was wondering how she managed such a feat when their eyes met.

Recognition passed between them, and Lady Shipton made her a small bow and would have passed on. But Georgie could not help herself from holding out her hand in greeting, saying that she was pleased to be able to speak to her again. On Lady Shipton's seeming mildly surprised, if pleased, Georgie said, "I cannot but feel that we did not thank you sufficiently for your kindness to us on the road."

After exchanging bows and greetings with Mr. Harding, whom she met with evident pleasure, Lady Shipton said, "A mere trifle. I am surprised you think on it at all."

Mr. Harding said, "If I may be so bold as to hazard a guess, having had the incident described to me, I think Miss Rowland means more than simply your kindness in sharing your parlour, but also your tact in removing yourself so promptly from the room, the atmosphere of which I understand Lady Rowland was making uncomfortably frigid."

Lady Shipton laughed. "Oh, that! Miss Rowland, let me assure you that your mother was not acting improperly, nor offending me in the least."

"I cannot agree with you," Georgie said, "but it is good of you to say so."

"You cannot know her reasons."

Mr. Harding said, "I assure you, she does. Not that Lady Rowland explained anything. But her uncle, Sir Henry Becknall, who is a most improper guardian of young ladies, did so in some detail."

"Dear me. Then you were not shocked, Miss Rowland?"

"Terribly, but I made a full recovery," Georgie smiled. "I am glad to have this chance to tell you that I do not share my mother's prejudice."

"Please do not be offended by what I am going to say now, Miss Rowland, but you are too young to be setting up your own opinion against your mother's."

"I am not offended at all, and think it kind in you to say so. But I have been setting my opinion against my mother's for many years now, and insist on being allowed to continue to do so, at least in some cases. I assure you I do not do so lightly."

Lady Shipton bowed and professed herself honoured.

Mr. Harding, who was on excellent terms with the lady, said, "Lady Shipton, you may be in a position to do Miss Rowland yet another favor."

Both ladies turned to him in surprise, but Lady Shipton said, "Naturally, I'd be pleased to do anything within my power."

"Miss Rowland's chief concern at the moment is with Neil Dandridge. If you can look without being seen to do so, you will observe him talking to a fair young lady."

"Yes, I see him. Is that not your sister, Miss Rowland?"

Georgie said, "Yes, Cecilia is my younger sister. This is her first Season, and she has proven to be more susceptible to Mr. Dandridge's charms than I care for. I have not yet found a cure for it."

"I comprehend completely. If I will not sound abominably vain for saying so, I think I can detach him from her side in such a way that it might discourage her."

"I'd be very grateful."

"Miss Rowland, I'd like to think that, in a way, we shall be friends. And between friends there is no use for things like gratitude. I will do what I can, for your sister's sake and for yours."

She moved off, and within minutes Georgie had the satisfaction of seeing Cecilia hiding her dismay and turning to smile on another young gentleman of her court as Mr. Dandridge walked off with Lady Shipton on his arm, giving no indication by his expression that he regretted his change of partner.

# Chapter 14

Lady Shipton was a shrewd woman, and one with a vast experience of the world. She also had a more particular knowledge of the habits of Mr. Dandridge. Therefore, although she was not normally an early riser, she startled her dresser by taking a morning ride in the Park for three days running.

She felt more than a little foolish--after all, why should she care about the fate of one of the many debutantes of this or any Season? Yet she found something to like about Miss Georgiana Rowland, something that appealed strongly to her and made her wish to further the acquaintance. It was rare for her to feel this way about a member of her own sex, so she was willing to help in what small measure she could with Miss Rowland's chief concern.

So she rode out, and on the third day, she saw what she expected to find. Miss Cecilia Rowland, riding a long-tailed grey mare, was *tête-à-tête* with Mr. Dandridge on his chestnut hack, without even the vestige of a chaperone. Worse, two of the greatest gossips in London were also riding their way, and had already seen the pair.

She spurred into a canter, leaving her startled groom behind a pace or two, and in a voice pitched to carry a long way without seeming shrill or loud, a skill that she retained from her days on the stage, she called out, "Miss Cecilia! I am *so* sorry to be late. Do forgive me. I know you were counting on me."

Cecilia did not have the wit to take her up, but instead stared at her blankly. Dandridge, however, who valued Lady Shipton's good opinion, at once said, "As you see, I have been protecting her for you. But I have no wish to get between two ladies determined on a snug gossip, so I shall leave you now. Miss Rowland, Lady Shipton, your servant."

As he rode off, Cecilia turned her fine eyes, blazing with indignation, to Lady Shipton. "I do not pretend to understand your purpose in approaching me, Lady Shipton--"

"Oh, do you not? I shall tell you. But pray, let us ride on." As Cecilia perforce let the mare match strides with her gelding, Lady Shipton said low-voiced, "I am attempting to save your reputation, you foolish girl."

Cecilia said stiffly, "I do not see how riding with you in the Park can be better for my reputation than an innocent ride with Mr. Dandridge."

"Oh, so you have claws, do you, little kitten? Draw them in and listen to me. Riding with me will not help you, but you are stuck with me until someone better comes along, so bear with it. If you do not comprehend the difference between riding with another lady, no matter who she is, and riding with a single gentleman while quite unchaperoned, then your education is sorely lacking! It bears every evidence of a clandestine assignation, and no matter how innocent it might be in intention and even in fact, the reality of our society is that, if it became known, it would brand you as *fast*. And nothing could be more fatal to your chances for a successful Season." Her voice sharpened. "How *dare* you do anything so vulgar, after all your sister and mother have done for you? To throw away their efforts on the whim of a moment is being ungrateful and undutiful in the extreme."

Cecilia's spirit was still high, but a flush stained her cheek. "There was no harm meant by either Mr. Dandridge or myself. We were private here, unseen by anyone."

"Then I assume you did not notice the Randall sisters, who are now directly behind us? No, do not turn to look. Just glance as if checking your saddle. Do you see them? They are London's most inveterate gossips."

"I detest gossips," Cecilia said savagely. "Mr. Dandridge and I simply wished a chance to speak to one another for half an hour without the constant interruptions of company, and that is all."

"Yes, I know what you wanted. And I know his arguments as well, every one of them."

"I do not understand you."

"I think you are beginning to. But let me elucidate. At a hazard, I would guess he has told you that his rakish past is behind him, but that the old tabbies in this town, all on far too high a form, refuse to acknowledge that he has changed. He told you that he has never met a girl quite like you, one who is unquestionably a lady, yet with a heart and mind liberal enough to understand him. He told you he is never so comfortable, nor can be so candid, as when in your company."

She had hit the mark. Cecilia's flush deepened. Lady Shipton went on, a little more compassionately, "I imagine he flattered your beauty, but not to excess, and complimented you on your mother and sister as well. But at the same time he insinuated that you are as superior to them, in your understanding and the tone of your mind, as is the moon to the stars. He then, probably over the course of several meetings, expressed dissatisfaction that the two of you were not able to converse as deeply as he should like, because you were continually being forced into the triviality of social conversations with all manner of people whom you both found dull and insipid."

Cecilia's expression was a mix of rebellion and acknowledgement of a truth she didn't want to hear.

"On another occasion," Lady Shipton guessed, "he ascertained that you rode out in the mornings--or, if you do not normally make a practice of that, he informed you that he did so. Most likely he arranged your conversation so that it was you yourself who suggested you might leave your sister and even your groom behind, just this once, and meet him here at such an early hour that you would never be seen by anyone of your acquaintance."

By this time, Cecilia's head was lowered in shame. Lady Shipton said, "Lift your head, child. We are still being observed."

The little chin came up, and her back straightened. "This... this is a habit with Mr. Dandridge?"

"Yes, I am afraid it is. Your virtue was quite safe, but Neil has a mischievous nature, one which delights in creating trouble. There have been many young women who have had to struggle to re-establish themselves in the ton, for one reason or another, because they happened to be pretty and charming, and had the bad luck to cross his path."

"I cannot believe he is so insincere," Cecilia averred stoutly.

Lady Shipton, exasperated, said, "Believe it or disbelieve, it means nothing to me. But do not tell me that, if you search your conscience, you are unaware that what you have done today is something to be ashamed of, should you have to confess it to your sister or mother."

"I will have to," Cecilia said unhappily.

More kindly, Lady Shipton said, "Not on my account. By calling out to you as I did, I made it clear to the Misses Randall that we had agreed to meet and that your being left alone was entirely my fault. I will not back down on that. If my word is your only problem, then you are safe, and need not distress your family."

This, however, turned out to be a false security, for at that moment a rider on a black horse came galloping toward them. Miss Rowland had discovered what Cecilia had done.

Georgiana's face was flushed and angry, and her hair and habit showed every evidence of her having dressed in a great hurry. "Cecilia! What have you been about?" she demanded as her horse plunged to a halt.

Lady Shipton said, "No, do not scold her, for I have already done so quite comprehensively, and she is very sorry. Are you not, Cecilia?"

Cecilia, now all tears, could only nod vigorously.

"And there was no harm done," Lady Shipton continued. "Or not much. Fortunately, I happened to be close by, and I joined Miss Cecilia before she was seen by anyone else to be alone."

"Alone?" Georgie repeated sceptically, glaring at her sister. But whatever else she might have said was interrupted by another person trotting toward their party. It was Mr. Winborne, and while Lady Shipton admired both his horse and his seat, occupying his attention for several useful moments, Cecilia dried her tears and composed herself.

Their party moved on, Winborne's simple nature being unable to discern how little his company was desired. The path narrowed and they divided, Mr. Winborne dropping back with Cecilia, seeing that she was out of spirits and trying to divert her. Georgie took the chance to say quietly to Lady Shipton, "Let me guess. Mr. Dandridge?"

"Do not be harsh with her. He is smooth and plausible and has much practice."

Georgie struggled with many uncharitable thoughts toward both her sister and Mr. Dandridge, but she conquered them and said with only a touch of acerbity, "I only hope this incident has cured her infatuation with him."

"If not, may I make a suggestion that will perhaps seal the issue?"

"You are all kindness, Lady Shipton. I would be grateful for any suggestion of yours."

"There is a young woman in your circle, a pretty but exceedingly timid girl by the name of Miss Emily Atwell. She has two older sisters, which should aid you in striking up their further acquaintance. I promise you that you will personally find it exceedingly dull, but if you are able to create an intimacy between Miss Emily and Miss Cecilia, it will be much to your sister's benefit."

"I know the Atwells, or rather, the eldest, Isabella. In what way would this acquaintance benefit Cecilia?"

"Miss Emily Atwell is a timid girl, but this flaw in her character is chiefly due to a broken heart, Miss Rowland. A heart broken by Mr. Dandridge in a cruel fashion. She is not the only young lady in town to bear this scar, but she is the only one who still seems to be wearing the willow, and who might, if tenderly coaxed, be willing to give your sister all the particulars of her sorrow. I am sure a clever girl like yourself can arrange matters so. Can you not?"

Georgie smiled. "I can and will. Once more I am grateful to you. Poor Emily!" She was lost in thought for a moment, but when Lady Shipton started to rein away, she said impulsively, "Would you please accompany us home and take some refreshment with us?"

"Your mother would not approve."

"As I have been reminded, the house is not my mother's, but my uncle's, and my uncle, I assure you, would have no objection at all. Please join us." When Lady Shipton made to demur yet again, Georgie's eyes sparkled and she said, "You need not worry about being snubbed by Mama, for she will not come downstairs for at least another hour. I must warn you, I am determined to further our acquaintance, so if you do not come, I shall call on you, and then you shall be forced to return the call or be considered impolite."

"Impolite! The thought terrifies me," Lady Shipton laughed. "But since our wishes coincide, and you press me so, then I will gladly accept."

# Chapter 15

Georgiana knew that her invitation to Lady Shipton was going to have repercussions, but she had come to a point where she felt that facing them squarely would show her heart and spirit in a better light than would avoiding them. Not for one moment did she think that Lady Shipton had coincidentally been riding in the Park at that early hour, and her gratitude was extreme. Had gratitude been her only emotion, however, she might have contented herself with a letter of thanks and with leaving her card at Lady Shipton's house. However, her desire from their first meeting had been to get to know Lady Shipton better, and every subsequent meeting with her had strengthened her conviction that, no matter what her past, Lady Shipton was a woman who possessed not only taste, elegance, and intelligence, but also a warm heart. To Georgie, these qualities far outweighed any indiscretions of Lady Shipton's youth, and for once in her life, her opinion was not going to be dictated by her mother.

Had she known exactly what the full extent of the repercussions would be, perhaps she would have quailed. But, much later, when she thought over the events of this momentous Season, she knew she would have--could have-

-acted no differently. However, at this point, she was unassailed by any doubts or premonitions.

Had Riddle been their butler in Grosvenor Street, he would have been their first obstacle, for she knew that the butler would have done his ineffectual best to bar the door against Lady Shipton. Addison, however, let them in with no sign of knowing who the lady was.

Mr. Winborne had left them in the Park, and Cecilia, as soon as they were within doors, excused herself and ran upstairs, most likely to have a good, heart-cleansing cry onto the sympathetic shoulder of Miss Puddleforth. Georgie felt sorry for her, but felt she'd learned a very hard lesson with little comparative pain, and she ushered Lady Shipton into the drawing room with every expectation of spending a pleasant half hour. Tea and cakes were ordered, and ordinary talk maintained until these were served and Addison and the footman had withdrawn. Then, to establish an immediate step toward intimacy, Georgie suggested that Lady Shipton's arrival so handily on the scene in the Park was no coincidence at all, and Lady Shipton furthered Georgie's pleasure by honestly acknowledging this.

Their friendship now well on the way to being assured, they spent a quarter hour in conversation that was marked by being not only varied but also sensible, during which parties and fashion were never once mentioned. This promising beginning was interrupted by Georgie's uncle, who, in his absent-minded way, wandered into the drawing room as he sometimes did, a book before his face. Hearing voices, he peered over the top of the book and said, "Oh, Georgie, I beg your pardon." Then he saw Lady Shipton. He stared, his mouth dropping open slightly, his mild blue eyes vacant of anything but a vague surprise. He removed his glasses and smiled. To Georgie, he said, "I see you have company. Will you present me?"

"Yes, of course! Lady Shipton, may I introduce my uncle, Sir Henry Becknall? Uncle Henry, Lady Shipton."

The proper things were said, and Uncle Henry, tucking his book behind him, bowed over Lady Shipton's hand. She asked curiously, "Becknall? Are you the same man who wrote the account of Trafalgar that was published last year?"

"You read it?"

"Indeed I did, and with great interest. You were not kind to those of us who have romantic notions of Lord Nelson, I must point out."

"I had no suspicion that a lady might read the book," he said, sitting opposite them, "or I would have been more tactful."

"It was quite obvious your emphasis was military. Still, I have had the battle explained to me many times, and never have I understood it better than after your analysis."

"You flatter me."

"No, I do not. If that were my intention, I would say that I now understand it completely."

"I hazard a guess that the political aspects were more comprehensible to you than the military ones."

"Yes, and I found your exposition on how the battle could have been avoided fascinating, even if you did skirt the issue of the personalities involved."

"I try to go lightly over heavy ground, ma'am," he smiled, and for the next ten minutes, Georgie was reduced to procuring tea for her uncle and listening with little comprehension to a lively conversation in which such terms as Whigs, Tories, Luddites, and reactionaries were thrown about, along with the names of the Prince Regent and much of his set, and others of the House of Lords with whom she was not in the least familiar. Lady Shipton brought it to a halt, observing apologetically, "We are prattling on and boring Miss Rowland, I am afraid."

Sir Henry looked conscious. "I am so sorry, my dear!"

"It does not signify," Georgie said, mollified by his sincere contrition, and unable to be annoyed with him at any event. "It is not often you meet anyone who understands you so well. I shall not forgive either of you for some time, however, for making me realize how ignorant I am. I, who pride myself on having an understanding superior to most of my peers!"

"You do," Sir Henry said, "but Lady Shipton and I are neither one of us your peers, but rather have many years of experience on you."

"Uncle Henry!"

Lady Shipton laughed. "I am not offended, fear not, Miss Rowland. I am not so vain as be concerned with concealing my age."

"You need not be," Sir Henry said, "since you know very well you do not look anything near it."

"Did I not just say I was not vain? I am not susceptible to flattery, either, and you shall not catch me out." She rose. "I have stayed long enough. Miss Rowland, my thanks for your hospitality, and no, please do not thank me yet again for such a trifling service. The pleasure was all mine. I would be delighted if you should call on me at any time, if you are allowed to do so. Sir Henry, thank you for a stimulating conversation. You have given me much to consider on my ride home."

When she was gone, Georgie went back into the drawing room, where her uncle was still standing, and said, "Does it seem to you the room is a little more dim without her?"

"Indeed, she is that kind of person. So are you, Georgie," he added with a smile. He picked up his book and settled his glasses on his nose, then took them off again. "You are off on one of your starts, are you not?"

"I am, I confess it. It seems vile to me to cut the woman, and for such a paltry reason, when she has done so much for us."

"It is not a paltry reason to a mother with innocent daughters to protect," Sir Henry pointed out mildly.

"That would be valid if Lady Shipton were vulgar, or inclined to tell us details of the more exciting parts of her life. Then no service she rendered us could incline me to do more than a letter of thanks. But she is the most interesting lady of our entire acquaintance. And I expect no argument from *you* on that score!"

He chuckled. "You will not get it. Georgiana, do you plan to stage this rebellion all on your own, or are you amenable to support?"

"I am quite amenable to any support, I promise you!"

"You know my opinion, and that I will not stint to give it, even to your mother. But I had something else in mind. Your mother has cried off from our party at the theatre tomorrow night, but insists that I still take you girls, and bring Mr. Harding and his friend--what is his name?"

"Mr. Winborne," Georgie supplied, resigned. Mr. Winborne's intellect was not of that order which would fix his name in her uncle's mind.

"Yes, Winborne. Why do I not send a card of invitation to Lady Shipton to join us? I hardly think the other gentlemen would object."

"That's a delightful idea! And no, they would not, for Richard likes her very much."

"Would Cecilia object?" Sir Henry asked with a significant look. "For I gathered that she was somehow involved with Lady Shipton's visit today, and that there might be some awkwardness."

"I am not sure," she admitted. "But I doubt it. Cecilia is fair-minded, and when she gets over this fit of the sullens, I am sure she will be delighted."

Sir Henry settled his glasses back on his nose and opened his book, but as he wandered away, he had one parting piece of advice. "I do not think I would mention it to Cecilia until just before we leave, and I would not mention it to your mother at all."

"Uncle Henry, you wicked man. You're encouraging me to deceive my nearest and dearest."

"Yes, I am, aren't I?" he said, his eyes twinkling. "But then your mother always did deprecate my influence on you, so it is all of a piece."

"You mean you can corrupt me with a clear conscience because Mama already says you do so? What kind of logic is that?"

"The logic is not lacking, only the ethics," he chuckled.

# Chapter 16

When they parted, Georgie went immediately upstairs to find Cecilia. As she expected, Cecilia had poured all her tears and troubles onto Miss Puddleforth's plump shoulder, the result of which was that she was more composed and less lachrymose. When Cecilia essayed on a stumbling apology, Georgie at once went to her, put an arm around her shoulders, and said, "Do not. Truly, I completely forgive you. The fault is mine for not warning you more explicitly about--"

Cecilia, however, shook her head vehemently. "You did warn me. I just did not listen. But I will from now on, I promise you. Whatever you say, I will do, exactly as you wish."

"If you go that far, I shall be most alarmed, and be certain that you are ill!"

"Am I so much trouble to you, then?"

Georgie sighed. This was going to be worse than she'd imagined. "You are no trouble, dearest. You're my sweet sister, and we will have no measuring of faults and troubles between us. Think on it--how would I know so many of the improper things to do, if I had not done some of them myself?"

"You cannot console me that way. I know very well that you learn from the mistakes of others. You often say so."

"And you must make the mistakes yourself. But it is not evil to make a mistake, Cecy, and that is all you did. Nor will you make it again, am I right? So we will put it behind us."

"Mr. Dandridge..." Cecilia began, but could not finish the sentence.

"Mr. Dandridge will say nothing, trust me. I doubt, in fact, that he will even avoid you, since his conscience gives him no particular qualms."

"Must I cut him?"

"I see the effect of his charms has not worn off you."

"He was very wrong to invite me to the Park as he did, but he meant me no real harm, as Lady Shipton herself said. And you will think me horrible, I suspect, but it adds greatly to my consequence to be seen to have attached him."

This guilty confession sent Georgie off into a peal of laughter. Hugging Cecilia, she said, "I never value you as I should. Yes, by all means, use Mr. Dandridge's attentions, if you will. He is, after all, a man of fashion and an excellent dancer, quite useful attributes. But, Cecy, you will not fall in love with him?"

"How could I? I saw at once, when Lady Shipton arrived, that he was annoyed at having his game detected, and not conscious of being in the wrong at all. I could never form a lasting attachment to a man with so maliciously mischievous a nature."

"Then all my worries are at an end."

"I must tell Mama what I did, however, and oh, Georgie, how I dread that."

"As for that, I have been thinking, and I believe it should not be mentioned to her."

"But I must! I cannot keep such a secret from Mama."

"Even when knowing it would grieve her? I am not suggesting that you lie to her. If she asks, you will, of course, tell her. But it is unlikely she will ever learn of it. Mr. Dandridge will not be anxious to spread the story, and Lady Shipton is discreet. As for the grooms, when I fetched my horse, I took care to mention that you had planned to meet me, but we had gotten crossed up and I was going to find you directly."

"I shall sink beneath my own guilt, when I see her."

"Do not puff yourself up so!" At Cecilia's startled look, she said, "You are making a major sin from what was merely a matter of a moment's poor judgment, and that, in its way, is most conceited of you. You would better serve me, our mother, and yourself if you were to pluck up, determine to learn from this experience, and walk out of this room as if it had never happened. When we go to the Afton's ball tonight, I want to see you in your best looks, smiling, dancing, and queening it over all those young men seeking a glance from your bright eyes. Do you think you can do that?"

"I feel that I should not. But if that is what you desire..."

"It most certainly is. I want to have a sister whose assurance and self-possession make me proud."

A watery smile moved Cecilia's soft mouth. "Then I will do my very best."

# Chapter 17

"Her very best," observed Mr. Harding that evening, as he brought Georgiana a glass of wine, "is not quite up to *your* standards, is it? I remember how, after you'd embarrassed yourself by accidentally driving up St. James Street in the middle of the afternoon, you went to your next party as if you'd done nothing more than tie your shoe in public, and laughed away everyone's criticism by frankly admitting your mistake. And that, you know, was much more shocking than what Cecilia did."

Georgie's fan, which she had been applying to cool her face, snapped shut expressively. "It was not!"

"Oh, come. If you were in your first Season this moment, would you prefer the Randall chits gossiping, or the significant looks you got from those members of White's who happened to be in the bow window when you drove past?"

"There is nothing to choose between them."

"There are two consequences laid before you, and hence, a choice. Do not try to argue with me, do not stick that little nose up in the air, and do not try to intimidate me with a scornful flash of your eyes. Choose, or admit you are irresolute and vacillating."

"Anything but that!" she cried in mock horror. "Very well, since you will have it, then I'd take the Randalls. But that is the last thing I plan to concede to you this evening."

"What, I have already used up all your concessions? I had plans to take you out onto one of the balconies and propose marriage to you once again. I am glad you warned me, so I did not waste my effort."

"You had no hope in that way, anyway. What, propose marriage to me after reminding me of my life's most embarrassing and humiliating moment, and pointing out that my sister's greatest foolishness does not equal my own? I would have been more likely to push you directly off the balcony, should you have done that."

"In that case, I shall save it for when we are on the ground. I have an even higher regard for my bones than for my dignity. But wait, I have a thought, which might save me. Should we become engaged, I can properly call Dandridge to account for his behavior."

"Challenge him to a duel, you mean? Would you do that?"

"Well... honestly, no, not even for you. He is a devilish good shot."

"Then there is no use in our being engaged."

"Alas, no. It was a promising thought, but I am sure I come up with another, if I bend my mind to it."

She laughed. "I am sure you will, for I have never yet known you to not achieve something, once you have determined on it."

Mr. Harding was insensibly cheered by this, although his cheer was as self-mocking as his previous humour had been. Until now, he had never regretted his enjoyment of the ridiculous or that he'd always shared it with Georgie. She believed she knew him too well to ever think him serious on this subject, and, with what he knew was arrant cowardice, he hesitated to make her realize it in an unmistakable manner. Before he let gloom chase away his momentary optimism, he changed the subject. "Now tell me, minx, what is your purpose in adding to our little theatre party?"

"I did not add to it, Uncle Henry did."

"You are not serious. Are you? You are. I must say, I thought Sir Henry the last man on earth to fall victim to the lady's charms."

"I think he rather fell victim to her intelligent appreciation of his book on the battle of Trafalgar."

"Nonsense. I have often given him intelligent appreciation of his works, and he has never once invited me to the theatre over it."

"You are quite a different case, however."

"Because I am not a beautiful woman?"

"Because he knows that, if you wish to come, you would have no scruple about inviting yourself."

"Little cat," he grumbled, and she laughed. "But I shall still observe him with great interest tomorrow night, and see if he joins the throng of those prostrate at her delicate feet."

She gave him a penetrating look. "Are *you* one of those, Richard?"

"Not I. I admire her greatly, but my preference is for another sort of woman entirely."

Did he imagine that she looked relieved? He dared not hope it, and if it were so, the look was instantly banished. She asked him, "Do you think me unwise to befriend her?"

"Unwise, yes, since you ask. You shall certainly regret it."

Her look was reproachful. "I expected better from you."

"Why? You asked me about the wisdom of your conduct. To fly into the face of your mother's expressed prohibition is foolish in the extreme. Remember, I know your mother!"

"You will always be splitting hairs! Very well, I shall rephrase my question. Do you disapprove of my doing it?"

"I could never disapprove of anything you do."

"Gammon! You often do. But tell me your opinion. You know I value it."

"My opinion, then, is that association with Lady Shipton will do you more personal good than social harm. Also that, since it brings her into my closest social circle--or will until your mother discovers it--I am delighted with your decision and approve unconditionally."

"I dread my mother's storms when she finds out," Georgie admitted, with a droop to her mouth that forced Mr. Harding to stifle an urge to take her into his arms and protect her from those storms and from anything else that could so disquiet her spirits.

"I shall call on you," he said, "and take some of her crochets onto myself. You know how I can send her up into the boughs with a single sentence. She will be too busy abusing me to have much breath to waste on you."

"That's noble of you, but I must decline. It exacerbates my temper to see her abuse you. Besides, if I am to take up lance and shield, I cannot then beg someone else to enter the lists for me. No, stay away, and leave me to deal with it. We are engaged for the Bracy's picnic in the afternoon of that day, so the more violent expressions of her displeasure will have to be of short duration. Are you invited to that affair?" she asked.

"I was invited, but declined."

"But it will be so enjoyable! The day promises to be a fine one."

"I can think of nothing so boring as to go out in crowded carriages, confined to the pace of the slowest horses, in the company of a score or more of people most of whom I cannot abide, all to spread out a blanket and a meal from which a multitude of insects must be diligently chased, and all to end with one lady or another fainting from the heat, or, more likely, the entire affair being rained upon."

"Did I not just say that the day would be fine?"

"You did so, but since you have not the management of the weather, that being one of the very few things you are content to leave in God's hands, I ignored your statement."

"You are the greatest beast in nature, and I do not know why I tolerate you."

"It does not say much for your taste in company, does it? Which reminds me, what scheme are you about with the Atwell girls?"

She affected innocence. "Scheme? I do not know what you mean."

"Do not try to pull the wool over my eyes. I am far too fly for your meagre talents of deception." She laughed, and he said, "I saw you greet Isabella Atwell so cordially that one would have believed you were bosom bows, yet I know your opinion of her is the same as mine."

"I did not know you had an opinion of Miss Atwell."

"I do have an opinion of her, if you care to hear it."

"I am all eager attentiveness," she said, fixing an appropriate expression on her features.

Mr. Harding's lips twitched. "Vixen."

She giggled. "Tell me your opinion, I beg you. I was not aware that you even knew her."

"I have endured the torment of standing up with her twice in my life. She is full of her own consequence, a consequence which I must say is all in her imagination, completely unsupported by birth, fortune, beauty, or accomplishments. She chatters endlessly about nothing, and adds to this an annoying, tittering laugh and a great deal of flirtation, of the variety that expects rather than requests admiration. Furthermore, she has not two original thoughts in her head to rub together."

"You are harsh!"

"Tell me you do not think the same, and I will modify my strictures." Her lips pinched together, but she did not speak, and he said, "Aha. You cannot."

"I have never been able to lie to you. You always find me out. But neither of us should be so odiously particular."

"I would agree, if our particularity was based on such things as a person cannot help, such as a lack of handsomeness or an unfortunate social position. But to base it on a person's character is not particularity, but judgment. Now, tell me what you are plotting." He waited, head tilted, but she returned a limpid, innocent stare. "You would be unwise to leave this to my imagination."

"This is true, because you are bound to put the worst possible interpretation on it. I was cordial--and no more than cordial! Do stop laughing at me!"

"I am not."

"Your eyes are laughing. I was *cordial* to Miss Atwell because Lady Shipton thought it would be a good thing for Cecilia to become acquainted with her youngest sister, Emily."

"Ah. That makes perfect sense."

"You know about Emily Atwell's unfortunate circumstance?"

"My dear girl, all the world knows. We are speaking of Neil Dandridge, after all, and what pleasure can he have with his games if no one else knows of them? Oh, do not look alarmed, I doubt he will publish Cecilia's indiscretion about. Between the pair of you, you and Lady Shipton have covered the ground well, and he does not want to be on Lady Shipton's bad side, either."

"Someone should give that man a sharp set-down."

"It would be salutary for him, but unlikely to occur. At least your scheme seems to have worked," he added, with a nod toward the end of the room, where Cecilia and Emily were standing, heads together, talking. Cecilia was vivacious, and Emily was looking at her with more animation than he'd ever seen the girl show. "I will give you this, Georgie. Your sister, for all her faults, has as good a heart as you possess."

"Better, much better."

"Since you persist in refusing my proposals, I will have to agree."

"You could try proposing to Cecilia. It is her sole ambition to be betrothed by the end of this Season."

"Thank you very much for your kind offer, but I have never had much taste for fair girls. Especially simple ones." He made a brief gesture to point out to Georgiana, "However, her refusal to dance in order to coax Emily Atwell from her shrinking silence has done her no disservice with her suitors. In fact, I will give you odds that at least one of them will now ask Miss Atwell to dance, in order to put himself up in Cecy's estimation."

"Why do you not do it?" she asked, turning to him suddenly.

"I?"

"Yes. And put yourself up in *my* estimation."

"Will you marry me if I do?"

"It would take more than one dance to bring that about. But I shall think the better of you."

"Very well, but only if you give me the waltz later."

She regarded him roguishly over her fan. "I was intending to save the waltz for a duke, or at worst, a marquis. But very well, I shall save it for you."

Mr. Harding, recognizing by the martial light in Georgie's eyes that she was off on another of her starts regarding Miss Atwell, did one step better than to solicit Emily for a dance. He dragged Winborne with him to make up a set with Cecy. While they were dancing, when Emily assumed, meekly, that he had only asked her to oblige Cecilia, he countered with a pretty compliment on her improved looks. This caused Emily to glow just a fraction more brightly, and gained him such a warmly approving look from Cecilia that he could all but feel the dagger-looks in his back from her less imaginative suitors. When Winborne, catching the idea if not the reason, then begged Miss Atwell for the next two, Mr. Harding felt his duty completed beyond even his darling Georgiana's exacting standards.

# Chapter 18

The evening at the play was one of the best evenings of the Season for Georgie.

Their party was swelled by one more, for Cecilia asked their uncle if she could bring Emily, and Uncle Henry was agreeable, if somewhat startled. Mr. Winborne had the pleasure of sitting between two charming young women whose appreciation of the play, like his, was restricted mostly to the comical parts and to the imaginatively staged battle in the second act.

Without having to concern herself with Cecilia's entertainment, Georgie was free to join in the conversation with Mr. Harding, Sir Henry, and Lady Shipton, which was carried on quietly during the comedic parts that engaged the attention of the other three and was about character, theme, and the social conscience of the playwright.

Sir Henry, although normally misanthropic, was always well-mannered when he bothered to bestir himself to go into public. But on this evening, he outdid himself. The ladies were treated to refreshment throughout the play and good society during the intermission. They suffered a very short wait for their carriage, and enjoyed an excellent light supper afterward, laid out ready for them at the Clarendon. If Sir Henry paid more attention to Lady Shipton than to any other lady, which he did, Georgie assumed this was either because Lady Shipton was closer to his own age, or perhaps because she was a newcomer to their circle, and that her uncle was simply extending himself to put Lady Shipton at ease. She found the latter idea amusing, for she was certain that a woman with such an air of well-bred confidence had never felt ill at ease in her entire life, no matter what the circumstances.

The next morning, Georgie entered the breakfast room to find only her uncle there, a book propped up before him, his attention so absorbed that it was astonishing his food ended up in his mouth and not in his lap. Each forkful was conveyed with an uncanny grace that owed nothing to his eyes, which, behind his spectacles, were moving rapidly back and forth, scanning the page. He wished Georgiana an absent good morning; she replied and added her thanks for the evening at the theatre, which he accepted even more absently. Smiling, Georgie helped herself to a substantial breakfast, and while she ate, she pondered what errand she could use to get her out of the house before her mother discovered what she'd done.

Her efforts, however, were wasted. While she was still drinking her coffee, Lady Rowland sailed into the room, and by the swiftness of her advance, the narrowing of her eyes, and the two spots of high colour on her cheeks, she was evidently in a temper. "There you are, Georgiana," she announced.

Inwardly, Georgie quailed, knowing that tone indicated her mother's most severe displeasure. But outwardly, she inclined her head and replied, "As you see, Mama. I am just finished with breakfast, and thought I would take Cecilia to the Pantheon Bazaar to find some coquelicot velvet ribbon for her riding habit."

"You will do no such thing. You are unfit to chaperone your sister, even to such a place."

For one brief, blissful moment, Georgie contemplated the pleasure of saying, *Very well, Mama, then you must bestir yourself and do it, instead of spending your days either with your bosom bows or invalidish upon your couch.* But she resolutely pushed the temptation aside and met her mother's glare with a curious look. "Am I? Why?"

"You know very well why! I have heard... oh, I can scarce say it," she moaned, sinking into a chair opposite Georgie. The footman stepped forward to serve her, and she dismissed him with a look. When he had closed the door behind himself, Lady Rowland turned to her eldest daughter with a barely controlled fury. "I have heard that you were seen in a box last night with That Woman."

"Goodness, it is not even noon yet, and we've had no callers. From whom did you have this news?"

"That is not important..."

"From Bridges, I suspect. Who heard it from another servant, who had it from a relative who works in a household in which one of the maids overheard the gossip of some ladies. Maybe the Bromleys, for they were both there and did bow to us."

"I said, that is not important! What is important is that you tell me, at once, how That Woman came to be with you!"

"She was invited."

"Invited? *Invited?* Have you lost your mind?"

To the surprise of both, Uncle Henry lifted his eyes from his book and said, briefly, "I invited her, not Georgiana."

"You stay out of this," Lady Rowland snapped. "I know very well who is behind it." Turning her fulminating glare on Georgie again, she said, "Bridges informs me that the woman actually *called* here, two days ago, and that you received her!"

"This is true. She did us a service, and I--"

"I do not care if she shod your horses with gold! A service! Pray, what service could she have possibly done you that you would admit her into my house?"

"It is Uncle Henry's house, Mama, and he did not object."

"It is I who am mistress while we are here, and you knew very well that *I* would object! In fact, I had expressly forbidden you to have any converse with That Woman. I could not have been misinterpreted. I was most specific."

"You told us that, should we pass her, we should acknowledge her with no more than a nod," Georgie agreed. "However, when she had been so kind to us, I took it upon myself to do more."

"You willfully disobeyed me!"

"Not willfully, Mama, no. But I did feel that, since Lady Shipton is received in most of the homes we habitually visit, it would be no cause for concern to show her a little more than common courtesy when she had done us a favor."

"What favor? How could you possibly have become indebted to That Woman in any way? Where would you have even seen her?"

"To answer the latter, I have seen her at four or five assemblies this Season. As to the former," she went on smoothly, her story already prepared, "Cecilia and I were accidentally separated on our morning ride, and Cecilia was approached most impudently by Mr. Dandridge. Lady Shipton sent him off and bore Cecilia company until I caught up."

"A likely story! That Woman, to be abroad on horseback at any hour before noon? You arranged to meet her there!"

"I did no such thing. I was completely surprised, since I, like you, assumed she was not fond of morning rides. But because she was so good as to step in when she had no reason to befriend us, simply from her kindness, I thought that to invite her to call was the least I could do."

"And I suppose next you will be leaving your card at Berkeley Square?" Lady Rowland said, quivering with indignation.

"I already have."

"Obstinate, headstrong, foolish girl! Will you ruin yourself and your innocent sister by willful association with a hussy?"

"Mama! She is no hussy, but a lady of character."

"She is nothing more than a common actress, a hussy who performed upon the stage and who--" She stopped, then continued after rewording her sentence, "Who has done things with which I would never dream of sullying the ears of a daughter of mine. Mutton dressed up as lamb! No matter how much money she has, she cannot hide her origins." She took a deep breath. "Perhaps I made a mistake in not explaining to you why I forbade you to associate with her, since, if you did not know, you could have no idea of why I am so adamant about it."

"But I did know, Mama," Georgie confessed. "I asked people about her. However, from what I have heard, she has led a perfectly respectable and blameless existence since she married the Earl of Shipton, and that was some fifteen years ago."

"She could go into a nunnery for fifteen years and still not be fit for proper society."

"This is what makes so little sense to me. A young man with the destructive tendencies of Mr. Dandridge, or a woman like Lady Orley, who is known to have broken the arm of one of her servants, are all received in polite society, but a woman such as Lady Shipton is not? As for her past, was it so bad? The circumstance of her being born into poverty and being forced to make her own way in the world can hardly be blamed on her, and as for the rest, well, I know of many society wives whose lovers far outnumber Lady Shipton's, and they have less excuse for taking them, and husbands to insult as well."

"How do you hear such things?" her mother demanded, then answered herself. "It is Richard Harding, I know it. I have long disliked his free ways of speech with you. He has no delicacy, no propriety."

"Such things are common gossip, Mama. But that is beside the point. I can name ten ladies, at least, to whom I would less want to introduce Cecilia, even if they are received by everyone."

"It is not for a chit of a girl like you to be setting your own opinions against that of society!"

"But I do not. Lady Shipton can be seen almost anywhere, and her parties are always well attended."

"Do you deny, then, that you have set your opinion against mine?"

Georgie blushed and lowered her eyes. "No, Mama. I did ask her to call, knowing you would disapprove. But, indeed, I hoped your opinion would be softened by the good office she did us."

"You thought no such thing! I know you and your intractability when you want to go your own way."

Georgie considered it wise to remain silent.

Lady Rowland said, "I can only be grateful that I have discovered this before it went too far. I am telling you directly, Georgiana. You are not to disobey me in this. You will not speak again to That Woman, and she will not be received in this house!"

At this, Sir Henry closed his book with such a loud noise that both ladies jumped in surprise and stared at him. When he pulled off his spectacles, they saw that his normally mild eyes were blazing. Lady Rowland flinched. Her brother was the most easy-going of men, spending so much of his life in his own mind that the frictions of the everyday world rarely tried him. But he did have a temper which, when fired up, could be extremely unpleasant.

He was definitely fired up now. "You forget yourself, Maria! You may set all the standards for your daughters that you please, but you will not set them for my home! Nor do I appreciate being subjected to a show of temper over my breakfast table!"

Lady Rowland rose in awful majesty. "Georgiana, come with me. We shall withdraw into the parlour."

"No, you will not," said her brother, rising with her. "Georgiana has acted appropriately with regard to Lady Shipton, and I will not have her further abused within my walls. What she will do otherwise will be her concern, and yours, but I will tell you to your head, Lady Shipton will be received here, and gladly."

"She will not!" Lady Rowland blurted indignantly.

"She will."

"You would ruin my daughters!" she said, and burst into tears.

"We only needed this, for you to enact us a Cheltenham tragedy! Ruin your daughters? Georgiana is correct--they are in less danger of being ruined by Lady Shipton than they are by some of the other women whom you so complacently admit here, such as the Countess Thierry, whose six children were all fathered by different men."

"Henry! Not in front of Georgiana!"

"Nonsense. Georgie is no bread-and-butter miss."

"You have no right to tell me how to raise my daughters!"

"I have the right. You are living in my home, and their dowries will primarily come from my coffers."

"You're a bachelor. You know nothing about raising girls."

"You are quite correct. But I will give you and Rowland this, you have instilled good morals into both of them."

With a glare at Georgie, his sister contradicted him. "We apparently failed with our eldest girl."

"Stuff and nonsense. Georgie acted with appropriate gratitude, in inviting Lady Shipton to call. Had some other woman aided her and Cecilia in such a way, and Georgie just shuffled her off with a thanks, you would have given her a rare trimming for being unpardonably rude."

"Lady Shipton is not just any woman."

"Quite right. She is an intelligent woman with delicate sensibilities. As for her calling again, you may be sure she will, for I have invited her myself. The issue is closed. If I hear about it again, Maria, I shall become angry." With that, he sat sharply down, settled his spectacles upon his nose, and opened his book again.

Georgie watched, fascinated, as her mother's face reflected her inner struggle. On the one hand, she felt strongly on the subject and, unaccustomed to being balked in anything, could not bear to have her authority over Georgie and the household so overthrown. On the other hand, her only recourse was to move her family to Rowland House, which was smaller, had no ballroom, was a goodly distance from being convenient to their horses, shopping, and socializing, and which, moreover, belonged to the current Lord Rowland, who would protest vigorously and probably profanely at having his contented bachelor life invaded by three women. While anger and frustration flitted across her face, she weighed the factors, and at last, admitting defeat, she swept out of the room, favoring both of them with a poisonous glare as the footman shut the doors.

Georgie let out a long breath. "Heavens, Uncle Henry. That was a superb rakedown."

He looked up from his book. "Hmm?"

She laughed. "I am astonished at the facility of your attention, to go within seconds from a roaring temper to complete abstraction. That must be a most interesting book!"

"Temper? I did not lose my temper." He regarded her over his pectacles. "You realize this is far from over, I hope."

"I do. But with you to back me, my courage is high."

He nodded and returned to his reading.

"You and your *my house* and *dowries*," she chuckled.

His lips twitched, but he gave no other sign of having heard her.

# Chapter 19

After such a pleasant evening at the theatre, and stirred to an even greater appreciation of his obstinate but right-minded little love for the way she was befriending Lady Shipton, Mr. Harding rose the next morning determined to make her an offer of marriage in such a way that even she could not mistake it for a jest. He had several ideas on the matter. He had a ring he could present to her, which he'd purchased at Rundel and Bridge, a pretty thing as delicate as her fingers. Not in common diamonds, either, but in sapphires to match her eyes. The little box had been sitting in a drawer in his dressing table since he'd bought it, but on this day, he might find the courage to bring it with him. Another scheme was more direct, being to get her alone long enough to explain to her in plain, simple, forceful language that she was most vehemently not his little sister any more. A third, which he naturally favored, was to take her into his arms and let a kiss convince her.

The way things were going, he believed he would need all three, and a bit of luck besides.

He dressed with care in a new waistcoat that had passed Elroyd's strict eye, coupling it with his best blue coat and dove-grey pantaloons, completing his apparel with shining Hessians and a sporty grey beaver. His cravat, tied in a deceptively simple fashion, which he'd copied from Mr. Brummell, was secured with a small diamond pin, and he wore no other jewelry except his watch and quizzing glass. "Being well dressed is the best first step to self-confidence," he said aloud as he set his hat at a precise angle between the conservative and the rakish.

"Quite so, sir," Elroyd agreed. He used a soft cloth to remove a spot from the Hessians whose mirror-bright gleam was a tribute to his skill, and gave the coat, which had been tailored for Mr. Harding's figure by the famed Weston, a final smoothing.

Mr. Winborne waited in the saloon, lounging at his ease. He was primed to occupy Cecilia's attention if necessary on this excursion, his task being to give Mr. Harding time alone with Georgiana. When Mr. Harding joined him, he heroically abandoned a half glass of excellent cognac, acceding to what he knew was his friend's nervous impatience, and he even went so far as to tell Mr. Harding that he looked bang up to the nines, an enthusiastic compliment which was received with a thin smile. Mr. Harding was already having doubts, and the tiny ring box felt like a piano crate in his pocket.

They were received in Grosvenor Street by Addison at his grumpiest, and instead of being taken directly to the ladies, were placed in the breakfast room, where they stared at each other in bafflement. Mr. Harding, who had never stood upon ceremony in this house and had no intention of doing so now, left Mr. Winborne and quickly, quietly ran up the stairs to the drawing room. He did not go in, however, for standing just outside the door, he heard the sounds of feminine voices raised in anger. Lady Rowland was giving Georgiana a rare trimming, and Georgie was giving it right back.

He could guess the subject, but he wanted no part of it, and went back down again even more quickly than he'd gone up. A moment after he rejoined Mr. Winborne, Cecilia came tripping in. "I am so glad you did not fail us, Richard!" she said dramatically, as if there had been a possibility he might. "There is such a to-do here today! I have not seen Mama so angry since the time Georgie and I dressed as boys to try riding astride."

Mr. Harding felt the hairs on the back of his neck prickle and stand upright, and by the expression of sheeplike terror on Mr. Winborne's face, he was feeling the same. "What is this all about?" he asked, as she gestured them to sit.

"Lady Shipton. I hope you do not object that I offer you no refreshment, but I--we--would really like to leave as soon as possible."

"Oh, bother the refreshments, Cecy. What about Lady Shipton?"

"Mama found out that Georgie called on her, and that she went to the theatre with us. It was *awful.* She came to my room and kept drooping over me, calling me her *poor darling* and going on and on as if Georgie were corrupting me! So then..." She blushed and lowered her eyes. "I made it even worse."

"I do not see how you could have," exclaimed Mr. Winborne.

"I do," said Mr. Harding. "You defended Georgie."

"Of course I did! But worse, I told Mama the truth about the other morning."

Mr. Harding grimaced. "Of course you did. Cecy, you really must learn to curb this tendency to blurt out everything."

"But Richard, I could not bear it that she kept comparing Georgie and me as if I were an angel and Georgie a demon!"

"And now," Mr. Harding retorted trenchantly, "she is even further confirmed in her opinion that Georgie's chaperonage has been too lax."

Cecilia wilted. "Yes. Even after I explained to her all the shifts I was put to, to get out of the house unobserved! She cannot dress Georgie down about Lady Shipton, not here, but she is taking her to task for everything else she can think of, even when the fault is mine."

Mr. Harding's brows rose. "Why is the subject of Lady Shipton denied her?"

"Uncle Henry said he'd send us all to Rowland House if Mama did not cease insulting Lady Shipton, and he strictly forbade her to speak to Georgie about it within his home. Georgie says he was quite magnificent," she added with simple pride.

At that moment the footman opened the door hastily, and Georgiana herself strode in, magnificent in her rage, her colour high and her eyes brilliant. She was dressed for walking in a blue pelisse, carrying a straw bonnet wrapped with blue ribbon, kid boots on her small feet. "Cecilia," she said, "why are you dawdling here? Get upstairs and dress at once, or you shall have to remain behind."

"You would not *dare* do that to me," gasped Cecilia, and made an exit of more speed than grace.

Mr. Harding's sweet love turned to him, and he at once abandoned all hope of this being the day that would see him happy. She was quivering with indignation, although she mastered it to greet them politely. "I am afraid you have come on a bad day, but I will not stand on ceremony with you. I will admit how glad I am that you did come. I think a few hours' contemplation of the beauty of Lord Elgin's marbles will do both Cecilia and me a great deal of good."

"I am sure it will," agreed Mr. Winborne politely. Mr. Harding realized he would no longer need Mr. Winborne's services, but he did not release him. He was not so kind, even to his closest friend, as to allow him to escape and leave him to soothe both young women alone.

# *Chapter 20*

While they were seated in the Rowland barouche, the presence of the groom prevented Georgiana from expounding on her wrongs, and by the time they arrived at their destination, the combination of Mr. Winborne's good-humoured charm, Mr. Harding's conversation, and the need to prevent Cecilia from turning into a watering-pot, had succeeded in restoring her spirits. She had a happy nature that could not bear either anger or resentment for long anyway, and her rapt contemplation of the famous marbles allowed no room for unpleasant thoughts.

Cecilia, whose nature was not so resilient, remained depressed and silent. Mr. Winborne eventually bore her away to a bench, where his attentions toward her comfort brought a sardonic smile to Georgie's face. When she and Mr. Harding had turned a corner and could no longer be seen by them, the latter remarked, "You're unkind to laugh at them, you know."

"I know it, and I do try to resolve myself not to. Mr. Winborne is all goodness, and Cecilia actually *likes* being treated as if she were a piece of fine china. But I would find it irksome in the extreme, so I must laugh. Or worse."

"Given your current mood, laughing is the alternative I choose," he said at once. Waving a languid hand at the marvels of Grecian art before them, he said, "Are you going to write poetry about these, or would you rather detail to me the heroic interventions of your uncle?"

"Uncle Henry!" she exclaimed. "He truly was magnificent." She quickly filled him in on the conversation over the breakfast table, omitting nothing.

Richard was praising Sir Henry in strong terms when from around another corner came the indirect subject of their discussion, Lady Shipton, on the arm of a tall, elegant young man. She checked when she saw them, as if unsure whether to greet them or simply pass by with a bow, but Georgie put out an impulsive hand to her. "Lady Shipton! Are you impressed by these works of art, or merely being fashionable by viewing them?"

"I am impressed, of course, and in no little measure by their very antiquity. Whatever one's opinion may be of the way they were obtained and brought here to England, I think it invaluable that they can be seen by those who, for one reason or another, can never personally witness the splendour of Greece."

"I must admit, that aspect had not occurred to me. I am simply in awe of them, and I appreciate their inspiration to our own arts."

The young man with Lady Shipton, with a respectful bow, said, "You speak of the poetry they've inspired?"

Lady Shipton, recalled to her duty, said, "Miss Rowland, will you allow me to present my stepson, Lord Shipton? James, this is Miss Georgiana Rowland, of whom I have spoken. And her friend Mr. Harding."

The two men exchanged punctilious bows. Lord Shipton, all affability, avowed he'd heard great good of Miss Rowland from his stepmama, which Georgie disclaimed. "But to answer your question, sir, I do not speak only of poetry. The classical Greek civilization, as represented by these monuments, has pervaded everything from sculpture to fashion, and all to the good, in my opinion."

"You prefer simplicity and flowing lines, then?"

"Who would not?"

The four continued on together, Mr. Harding dropping back to offer his arm to Lady Shipton, with whom he carried on a desultory conversation with only a small part of his mind. The rest of it was taken up with the spectacle before him of how an accomplished flirt with an intelligent mind could bring out the best in Miss Rowland. Lord Shipton was obviously disposed to admire her in every way, and while Mr. Harding was sure his lordship's complacency would not survive one of Georgie's blistering set-downs, or, worse, being laughed at by her, he still could not view the way she looked up at Shipton, eyes sparkling and lips smiling, with any degree of comfort.

Nor did he get comfort when, having separated from Lady Shipton and her stepson, and going to rejoin Mr. Winborne and Cecilia, he remarked that she had seemed to enjoy Shipton's company. She heard the bitterness in his voice, but misinterpreted it. "I did enjoy his company," she said. "He is not only charming, but has a great deal of good sense. He seems to have taken his father's remarriage completely in his stride, and is very fond of her. I cannot help but like such a man. But are you irritated with me for abandoning you? I thought you would be tolerably entertained by Lady Shipton. I know you enjoy her company, and had not thought you could be bored."

With her earnest gaze on his face, what could he do but dodge the truth entirely? "I was far from bored," he said. "I am simply wondering if I shall now fall into your mother's disfavour, as not only did I not bear you forcibly away from the evil company of... what is it she calls Lady Shipton?"

"*That Woman,*" Georgie grinned.

"Yes, the evil and corrupting company of That Woman, but I also allowed you a good half hour *tête-à-tête* with her son. When Lord Shipton proposes marriage to you, and you become That Woman's daughter, your mother will wash her hands of you and blame the entire thing on me. I naturally have some qualms about the entire affair, since hitherto Lady Rowland and I have had the most cordial of relations."

"Most cordial," agreed Georgie with a chuckle. "You are quite right, she would lay all the blame on your shoulders, so I shall refrain from running to her the moment we get home and informing her of my transports of delight at having met Lady Shipton while viewing the marbles with you."

"Excellent idea. Lady Rowland can only handle a certain measure of pleasure. We do not want to overwhelm her."

Georgie agreed with a prim face, but could not maintain it, and laughed again. "Abominable man. You teach me disrespect for my Mama."

"In that, I am in excellent company, since your uncle seems to be doing likewise."

"I know. It is awful. I feel that I should be sunk with guilt, but instead I am filled with triumph and a conceit of my own opinions. You must bring me to earth with a recollection of the duty I owe my Mama, and give me a good raking down for being a disobedient daughter."

"You're a wicked, disobedient girl," he said promptly, and with no tone of censure at all in his voice. "There, was that satisfactory?"

"Entirely. I am now filled with contrition for my behavior. I shall reassure you on one point, at least, which is that Lord Shipton will not make me an offer."

"How can you be so sure?"

"I am not *green*, Richard. He is disposed to admire me, but that is all." Casting him a roguish look, she said, "I see that it is not only a woman whose *imagination is very rapid; it jumps from admiration to love, from love to matrimony, in a moment*."

"Oh, no. If you are going to quote to me from novels, I am done with you."

# Chapter 21

On Wednesday morning, Lady Rowland called Georgiana to her sitting room to discuss their coming evening at Almack's. That esteemed and exclusive establishment was too elevated, and Cecilia's success there too important, for Lady Rowland to risk even the slightest impropriety in the behavior of her daughters, and her desire was that Georgiana would stay at home that evening. "Heaven knows what you would be about. Encouraging Cecilia to flirt with every rattle and half-pay officer, no doubt."

"Mama!"

"I am sorry if I seem harsh, but lately I hardly feel I know you. You, my own daughter. A most uncomfortable sensation, I assure you. Where once my trust reposed without a qualm, now I must weigh and measure."

Georgie bit off what she wanted to say. Primly, she said instead, "I am very sorry you feel that way, Mama." Truthfully, she did not mind being excluded from this prime treat, for while she knew how vitally important to Cecilia's success was her acceptance at Almack's, Georgie was always bored there.

When she'd extricated herself from her mother's sitting room at last, having endured another ten minutes of recrimination, she went downstairs to the drawing room to go through the stack of invitations on the desk. Not every hostess was a slave to Almack's, only every hostess with an unmarried daughter, so there were several invitations for that evening which, before, she'd been obliged to decline. Included in these was an invitation to one of Lady Shipton's literary evenings, and that party was a sore temptation. She had to put them all aside, however. It would do her no good to send word that now she was free to attend. She could not go unescorted.

She was sitting there with the invitation cards spread before her, her chin in one hand and a glum expression on her face, when her Uncle Henry entered the room. He had the ubiquitous book before his face, and sat and read for some minutes before he even noticed her presence. When he did, however, he put one finger on his place, looked at her over his spectacles, and asked her what was the matter. She explained. Sir Henry listened without interruption, then said, "You wish to go to Lady Shipton's."

"Indeed I do. You know my tastes. I would much prefer it to Almack's."

"So I should think. I have never set foot in the place, but by all accounts, it is universally insipid."

"I did not think so, my first Season."

"No, because its reputation is such that, I am sure, you believed some young and handsome fellow would come up to you, ask you to dance, fall deeply in love with you by the end of the set, and propose to you before a month was out."

She had to smile. "Something like that."

"Almack's is an abominable bit of conceit on the part of a few women, all of whom are proud, some of whom are haughty, and most of whom have no reason to be either one. Exclusivity is the shortest route to popularity, but far from the best. And Almack's has only a large ballroom and exclusivity to recommend it, the music being only tolerable, the rules autocratic, and the food atrocious."

"Uncle, you waste your breath. I am in complete agreement with you."

"Then if you should go to Lady Shipton's, you would not spend the evening pining away for the dubious delights of an evening at Almack's?"

"How absurd you are! No, I would not pine for an instant. But why dream about such a thing? I cannot go."

"Cannot, or will not?"

"Cannot. I have no escort."

"And that is your only objection?"

"That is enough."

"I have received an invitation and plan to go. Richard, also, and he is to take me up in his carriage. Correct me if I am wrong, for I am, after all, a bachelor, and unversed in the niceties of feminine behavior, but would not your uncle's escort be sufficient?"

So much pleasurable excitement filled her that she bounced from her chair. "Oh! Uncle Henry! That would be most acceptable!"

"Then we shall go," shrugged her uncle, and, oblivious alike to her joy and her thanks, went back to his book.

So it was that, after seeing Cecilia dressed and in her best looks, and having kissed her a fond goodbye and bid her to enjoy herself, Georgie skipped merrily back upstairs, where she was helped into her blue satin gown with the silver spangles and gauze half dress by a disapproving Puddles. She was back downstairs in good time to be handed into Mr. Harding's carriage by her uncle.

Lady Shipton's home was in a good part of town, but was, as the lady herself would admit, not large enough for a proper ball. By dint of inspired planning, however, it was exactly suited to the kind of parties she preferred. Her servants prepared every public room in the house for a different use, and those who attended could play cards, if they so desired, or listen to music or to readings, or dance, or watch amateur theatricals, or even simply hold intelligent conversation over excellent food and drink, all in one evening.

Lady Shipton herself moved always among them, never seeming harassed or hurried, yet managing to assure herself of the comfort and enjoyment of every guest. She was ably seconded by her butler, a volatile genius named Ardmore who was at his supremacy in affairs of this nature. No guest was ever bored or alone at her parties, unless they wished it so.

Georgie, clinging to her uncle's arm and feeling both elated and overwhelmed, was greeted by Lady Shipton with unaffected delight. Her apologies for her last-minute acceptance of the invitation were brushed aside as nothings, and she was recommended to visit the front drawing room. Leaning forward conspiratorially, Lady Shipton said, "Lord Edgebury is reading his chivalric poetry dedicated to his imaginary, unattainable lady-love. That will, I believe, please your sense of the ridiculous. But after him is a young man named Worthen, who, despite an unprepossessing appearance, writes about Nature in a quite beautiful way."

Without exactly knowing how, she got separated from her uncle, but Mr. Harding stayed at her side, and although she regretted her uncle's absence when the full glory of Lord Edgebury's flowery tributes burst upon her, she still had Mr. Harding to appreciate the absurdities. In the interval, when he escorted her to get refreshment, she could barely wait until they were out of earshot before bursting into giggles.

"I was afraid you would do that, right on the spot," Mr. Harding said dryly.

"Oh, no, I would not be so rude. But it strained my self-control, I assure you."

"I could tell. Indeed, there was one point where I feared to meet your eye, out of certainty that you would not be able to contain yourself."

"I think I know the place. *But lilies droop in water pure...* oh, what was the rest?"

"*And mirrored, know they fail, Their grace not yours, their faces only pale,*" he quoted with deep solemnity.

Her giggles returned. "Oh, you are too bad. You should not encourage me to make fun of such an earnest poet. But you remembered it so exactly?"

"On purpose, knowing you marked it."

"Wicked, delightful man. I must get a copy of that poem for my uncle."

"If you do, accept a gentleman's advice and do not give it to him over breakfast. It would be injudicious and unfair, and quite ruin his digestion for the day."

"I will take that under advisement. Let us go back, for this next poet, Lady Shipton says, is worth hearing."

"Only if you promise me a dance afterward, so that I am not made stiff from so much sitting."

"My hand on it," she said.

Mr. Worthen was a small, thin, diffident man, not quite thirty years of age, dressed neatly rather than affecting the picturesque attire of Lord Edgebury. Georgie felt she might have passed him on the street and never marked him, and indeed, perhaps she had. But once he had cleared his throat a few times and begun his reading, she knew she would never forget him. His poetry was as delicate and strong as the natural subjects it described, full of darkness and colour and brilliant light, the words and rhythm exalted yet approachable. Her applause, and her acceptance of his card so that she could send for a copy of his poems, were both from sincere appreciation.

After that, however, ready for a change, she looked about for her uncle. Sir Henry was in the music room, listening to one of the female guests playing the harp--quite well, actually--with Lady Shipton for a companion. Feeling he was being well entertained, Georgie therefore had no qualms about skipping upstairs to the ballroom to fulfill her promise to dance with Mr. Harding.

When the first set was done and they were sitting while she cooled her face with her fan, another acquaintance of hers came to her side. Lord Shipton expressed himself pleased to see both of them, and offered to introduce them to other eligible partners. He claimed Georgie for the second waltz, yielding reluctantly to Mr. Harding's previous claim to the first. Thanks to his efforts, despite her having few acquaintances in this social group, Georgie never lacked for a partner.

# Chapter 22

Georgiana got home well after the Almack's party, naturally, but since she'd left word with Addison that she was attending a party with Sir Henry (without saying which one), she assumed her mother and sister would be abed and asleep when she returned. Her mother was, although Addison informed her gloomily that Lady Rowland had been displeased to find her from home.

Cecilia was also in bed, but not asleep. Instead, when Georgie had doffed her finery, gotten into her nightgown, and slipped silently into the bedroom, she found Cecilia sitting up, her expression miserable and her face bearing all the marks of a girl who has just enjoyed a long cry.

"Cecy!" Georgie set her candle on the table and sat on the bed, taking Cecilia's hand in both of hers. "Why are you so sad? Did something unpleasant happen at Almack's? No, surely, that's impossible."

"Not at Almack's. Not exactly, anyway. I mean, we were there, but it had nothing to do with the dancing."

"But something happened. Please tell me."

"I will," Cecilia said. "But I hate to. I feel so low, Georgie."

Georgie put an arm around her. "Just tell me. You will feel the better for it."

Cecy sighed, laying her head on her sister's shoulder. "To begin with, Mr. Dandridge asked me to dance."

"Dandridge? He is allowed into Almack's?"

"His mother is the sister of a duchess, Mama says, and his manners are pleasing, so he is welcomed everywhere. Which just goes to prove all that you have told me about the hollowness of society," she added in a depressed manner.

"Never mind my social commentary," Georgie said briskly. "What did Mr. Dandridge do to upset you, my dear?"

"Nothing! He was all courtesy and charm. Indeed, so pleasant was he that I began to think I had been too severe on him in my thoughts on what passed between us in Hyde Park. But then, when I decided to sit out the next dance, I could not find Emily anywhere. I searched for her, thinking she might need help with a pin, and found her in an alcove, all but hidden by a plant. Since I could not coax her forth, I sat with her, because she looked most distressed. She did not want to speak of her trouble, but I pressed her, because I could not bear to see her so unhappy. And... she told me."

"About her connection with Mr. Dandridge?"

"You know about it?"

"Only rumor, and very little of that. I'm sure you know more. Was it told to you in confidence? Or can you tell me?"

"She did not speak in confidence, because she was sure I knew, as everyone else does, or so she believes. But I never heard the story. And really, there is not much to it. When Emily first came out, she was so shy that no one, even her nearest and dearest, believed she would take. But Mr. Dandridge noticed her and made her the object of his gallantry. Indeed, he singled her out with such partiality that, for a short time, she was quite the rage, since some part of society tends to follow where he leads. His attentions were most particular, so pronounced that her mother expected an offer any day. And as for Emily, she was completely head over ears in love with him. She felt as if she were in a fairy tale, with herself as the modest heroine picked from obscurity by a handsome prince. If you could have but seen her face when she told me this, Georgie! Even now, with all that has passed, she looks back on it as the happiest time of her life."

"I take it that Mr. Dandridge did not make her an offer."

"Worse than that. For no reason, with complete abruptness, he dropped her acquaintance and moved on to another lady. When Emily went to a ball and he did not at once appear to ask her for a dance, she sought him out, and--the *odious* man! He pretended he'd forgotten her name! He treated her with cold indifference, and when she turned away, before she'd gotten quite out of earshot, she overheard him give her name to the gentlemen with whom he was talking, and describe her as a country dowd with little fortune and less countenance. Her heart was quite broken." A sympathetic tear trickled down Cecilia's cheek, but her chin squared and her eyes burned with a martial fire. "I wish I were a man. I would challenge him to a duel and run him through!"

Hiding her pleasure at how well Lady Shipton's advice had worked, Georgie said, "I almost wish you were, and I would be your second. How fortunate Emily is to have your friendship!"

"She is the dearest, sweetest girl. He must be the greatest beast in all creation, to have treated her so shabbily. And it gets worse, Georgie!"

"How could it get worse?"

"Emily heard later that all his attentions to her were due to a wager. He boasted to a friend of his that he could bring any decent young woman into fashion, and his friend bet him that he could not. He chose Emily to prove his point, and his friend agreed. Once the bet had been won and paid, then he had no more use for her."

This shocked even Georgie. "I have never heard anything more vile."

"I wish there were something we could do about him!"

"You can be assured that we will watch for any opportunity, and if it arises, we will take advantage of it. Although I fail to see anything immediately offering, one never knows."

# Chapter 23

Mr. Harding, taking Georgie for a drive to Richmond Park the next day, was the recipient of all this information. When Georgie's anger had finally wound down, he said mildly, "I hope you do not expect me to stand in for Cecilia and challenge the fellow. I will not do it. Dueling is quite out of fashion."

"No, of course not. But you are a man--"

"I'm so pleased you have noticed!"

"Stop being difficult and listen to me. You are a man, and therefore have means to get information about another man that are quite beyond my scope. If you learn anything I can use against him, will you tell me?"

"I will not."

She stared at him. "You will not?"

"No, I will not. Do not glare at me. Think for a moment. I know that when you are in a rage, this is difficult for you, but do try."

"I am not in a rage."

"Have I let you take the reins?"

"No," she admitted.

"Since I myself taught you to drive, you know that I have no prejudice against having you drive my horses. And you normally do. So why do you think I have not yet offered?"

Her cheeks flamed. "You think I will jib their mouths out of impatience."

"Which you always have done, when you are in a rage. I have seen you like this before, and while the state is most becoming on you, especially when for a righteous cause, that does not mean I shall enter into it with you. Consider, first, that despite our close relationship, we are not actually related."

"That's true," she conceded, sulking.

Mr. Harding struggled to keep his countenance. He needed to be serious, but it was difficult when she pouted so adorably. "Secondly, neither you nor Cecilia are in any way related to Miss Emily Atwell. While I applaud your heart, it leads you into improper paths in this case."

"I shall at least give him the cut direct!"

"If you wish to look foolish, by all means, do so."

"Foolish!"

"Everyone will say you do it because you are piqued that he has decided you are unworthy of his attentions. He will be the first to say so, as well."

There was a long silence. Mr. Harding settled his horses into a quiet walk and waited for her to speak again.

Georgie looked up. "Maybe I can do the same thing to him that he did to Emily!"

"You are a monstrously pretty girl, Georgie, but that will not serve. He is far too clever, and unlike Miss Emily, he has no heart to lose."

"You are right. But I will not be happy if I cannot do *something*. Have you no suggestion at all?"

"Not that occurs to me. But then, my interest in the subject is minimal."

"How can it be? You are not so heartless."

"Emily Atwell is all but a stranger to me. I care about her only to the degree that she affects your happiness."

"But my happiness is affected!"

"Cecilia's is."

"And therefore mine!"

"You know, if you accepted my offer and became engaged to me, I would have more justification for interfering," he ventured, more from a spirit of endurance than with any hope.

"You sound like a villain from a melodrama. *Marry me, my dear, and I vow I will not turn your family out of doors and raze your childhood home to the ground.*"

He shouted with laughter. "Oh, very well. I will see what I can do. I promise nothing, however, not even to try hard."

This satisfied her.

Over the next few weeks, as Easter came and went with all its attendant celebrations, Georgie's life settled into something like a routine. Her only true excitement was that Mr. Harding informed her he had a plan of action against Mr. Dandridge, which involved Lady Shipton, but which he refused to describe to her until it reached fruition. Lady Shipton was equally reticent, although more kind in her expression of refusal, not wanting Georgie to get her hopes up.

Cecilia's sincere pity for Emily Atwell led her to champion the girl in the only way she could, by noticing her at every ball and party. The two became friends, and Georgie saw, with a tang of regret, that her place as the primary confidante in Cecilia's life was gradually being taken by another girl.

She continued to pay occasional calls on Lady Shipton, but Lady Shipton never again called at Grosvenor Street, saying with great delicacy of feeling that she did not wish to disregard the wishes and scruples of Lady Rowland, even for the pleasures of Georgie's company. Georgie accepted this with grace, honouring Lady Shipton's wisdom. In emulation, she presented a more demure and obedient front to her mother, and Lady Rowland gradually set aside her vexation and admitted Georgie at least partially into her good graces again.

Her Uncle Henry remained her co-conspirator. In fact, where once he could almost always be found at home of an evening, he began to go out and about a great deal more. Only Georgie and Mr. Harding noticed that he was invariably, and solely, to be found at any function that Lady Shipton was attending. Lady Rowland, completely unsuspicious, assumed his new activity was in deference to herself.

Mr. Harding did not propose again, and as she had never once thought to take him seriously, Georgie did not notice. Much of her time and attention was being agreeably taken up by Lord Shipton, whose attentions were becoming marked. No longer did Georgie think he was merely enjoying an idle flirtation. He let it be known that he found her beauty much to his taste, her manner pleasing, and her company enjoyable. Whether more would follow remained a mystery, and, although Georgie did not know it, an agony to Mr. Harding.

Mr. Dandridge, that Nonpareil amongst the Corinthians and inveterate gamester, had a reversal of fortune. He accrued gaming debts so deep that he was forced to leave the country and go to France to avoid them. Mr. Harding let Georgie know that this ill luck was due in large part to himself and Lady Shipton, and Georgie and Cecilia were both most grateful to them. Emily, without the dread of always seeing Mr. Dandridge at parties and balls, began to bloom. She would always be timid, but now her shyness was no longer a fault but rather a becoming feminine modesty, and when seen everywhere with the vivacious and gregarious Cecilia, she enjoyed a renewed popularity, humble, but completely to her taste.

At the midpoint of the Season, Lady Castlereagh threw the biggest ball of the Season. Georgie enjoyed herself there without a shadow of trouble on her mind. She had no idea that it would be the last day she would do so for some time to come.

# Chapter 24

The day after the Castlereagh's ball, Lady Shipton welcomed a morning caller at an unusually early hour. The gentleman sent up his card but, rather than just leaving it, requested an interview with her, if it should suit her convenience.

Glancing at the name, she agreed, had Ardmore show him into the drawing room, finished her *toilette* without haste, and went down to see what Sir Henry Becknall wanted with her. She suspected it had something to do with the Dandridge affair, although whether his reaction would be positive or not, she had no way of guessing. Since she was a woman who preferred to get over heavy ground as quickly as possible, she said, after giving him her hand in greeting, "If this is about Mr. Dandridge, Sir Henry, then I am sure Mr. Harding has already given you my thoughts."

Sir Henry seemed mildly surprised. "No, it is not. What about Mr. Dandridge? Did *you* have something to do with that, ma'am?"

"A great deal. And yet I need not have confessed it! What will you think of me now?"

She gestured him to the chair by the fire, and as he sat, he said, "I would never think ill of you. But I fail to see how you could have influenced Dandridge to make so drastic a change in his circumstances."

"Nothing could be easier." Ardmore entered, and she offered Sir Henry tea, which he declined, and wine, which he accepted. When Ardmore was gone again, and the doors closed against the curiosity of the servants, she met his brightly interested gaze and said, "Truly, Mr. Dandridge has many weaknesses, any one of which could have been exploited. I simply aided in this particular instance in my own small way."

"And that was?"

"You question a lady, sir?"

"You know I have a lively curiosity, ma'am, and particularly where you are concerned."

"You shall think me very wicked."

"I think I can promise not."

"Very well then, I shall tell you. Mr. Dandridge is, by habit, somewhat lax in matters of play and pay. He recently had an excessively ill run of luck. I have influence in certain quarters, so I was able to assist this misfortune. With quarter day a long way off, he was dependent on the good will of those who held his vowels. Unfortunately for him, they were all bought up by someone who did not wish him well."

"By you, ma'am?" he said, astonished.

"By me, through the good offices of the industrious Mr. Harding. In fact, I came down this morning believing that you were going to be tiresome and demand that I disclose the entire sum to you, so that you might repay me."

"An offer, I assume, that you would have refused."

"Certainly. It was not a trifling amount, it is true, but I can easily afford it."

"I am glad you do not attempt to come over on me by expecting me to believe a *trifling amount* would send a man out of the country! But you would not. I believe that lies are abhorrent to you."

"Lies have served me well in my life," she corrected him gently. "But when I married Shipton, I put them aside, and now, yes, they are abhorrent. I tell you truthfully, therefore, that I would not have a delicacy of feeling on your part rob me of my pleasure in being of assistance to your nieces."

"I would rob you of nothing which gives you pleasure," he said.

Something in his tone, an unusual warmth, made her study his face more closely. He looked much the same, a square-faced man, pleasant-looking if not handsome, his uneven features given liveliness by the bright, inquisitive, piercing intelligence in his eyes. "I am grateful to you. Then what is the reason for this visit, Sir Henry?"

"I have an offer of another kind entirely, and one which, should you be so kind as to accept it, would make my suspected errand superfluous. In fact, it is not truly an offer, but a boon that I ask. I..." A man of many words, at this most important time in his life, he stumbled and said, with clumsy candour, "I wish to beg you to give me your hand in marriage."

Lady Shipton had received many offers from besotted gentlemen since her widowhood, but never one of marriage. She was not entirely surprised, since Sir Henry's attentions had been marked and he did not have the reputation of being a flirt. But she had always assumed that his affection was one of infatuation, and he was such a normally reclusive and sensible man, she'd been sure that he would eventually fade out of her life. It seemed, however, that Sir Henry's wish was quite the opposite. "I am not sure what to say," she admitted.

"Sparring for wind, or seeking a polite negative? If the latter, please do not feel you must stand upon ceremony with me. I know I am not the most promising sort of man for a woman to marry."

"I am sparring for wind, sir," she said, and saw his face, which had fallen despite his attempt to maintain a calm exterior, brighten again. "Although I should not admit to knowing what such dreadful cant actually means!"

"That is one of the reasons I love you. You know it, admit it without blush, and yet lose not one jot of your elegance."

"You love me?" That did surprise her.

"Why else would I propose marriage?" he asked, even more surprised.

"In our society, there are many more reasons."

"Ah, I see. I lost my entire fortune upon 'Change and must instantly recoup. Alas, in that case, what a pity that you have depleted yours in the cause of disgracing Mr. Dandridge."

She tried not to laugh, but failed. "Obviously that is not a reason."

"No, it is not. Nor do I need a housekeeper. I have a perfectly good one. Nor do I need a mother for my children. I have none. I do not need a lady to accompany me to parties, as I rarely go out. And while you are beyond doubt the most beautiful woman I have ever seen, I realize that my opinion in that matter is biased, and that there must be some diamonds of the first water who may, when viewed with an objective eye, be considered more beautiful. I wish to marry you because, in this time I've grown to know you, my admiration for you has deepened into love, and the thought of spending the rest of my life with you fills me with complete joy. That is all."

"All? That is everything." Overwhelmed, she rose and went to the window, looking out blindly, her hand toying with the sash cord. "Sir Henry," she said at last, without turning to look at him again. "I confess I am surprised by this offer. Nor do I wish you to think me insensible of the honour." She turned then, and saw that his expression was a unique mix of amusement and despair. "I believe you have not considered everything about me, in asking me to be your wife."

The amusement immediately won out. "Do you speak of your past?"

"I do, sir. You must know that it is not what a well-bred man wishes of the woman to whom he gives his name."

"Of course I know it. My sister has dinned it into my ear. I fail to see how that is significant."

"If so, you are a more remarkable, or more foolish, man than I have ever before met."

"With the exception, perhaps, of Lord Shipton?"

She smiled at the memory of that amiable, besotted, devoted peer. "With that exception, yes."

"May I be completely candid, ma'am?"

"I wish you would."

"Then allow me to point out that I am not such a man as Lord Shipton was. I had a respect for his good nature, but his understanding was not deep. He loved you, but I doubt you loved him as deeply in return. I do not see how you could, for he was far beneath you in many ways. You married him to establish yourself in society, I believe, and in fact that may well have been your goal for much of your life."

"You do not find such cold ambition repulsive?"

"I would, were it cold. But you struck a bargain with Shipton, did you not? He would give you everything you needed to find a place in his society, a society to which you were much more suited than that which you had been born into, and in return, you would be a devoted, faithful wife who would dedicate yourself to his happiness. Am I wrong?"

Astonished, she said, "You see far more than you seem to, Sir Henry."

"Perhaps. Although it is not so much a matter of perception as deduction. I will add that Shipton, in the few times I saw him, seemed to be a very happy man."

"And now you propose a similar bargain with me?"

He frowned, although the amusement still in his eyes made it a mock severity. "You are far too intelligent to think so. Your place in society is assured. You can rise no higher, since the tabbies who still forbid your company are such high-sticklers as would continue to be obstinate even if you married the Prince Regent himself. By marrying me you will indeed take a further step toward respectability, since my reputation is considerably less tarnished than Shipton's, but you would also descend from being the widow of an earl to being merely the wife of a knight, and your freedom and brilliance as a hostess must be somewhat dimmed by marriage to a man famed for his reclusiveness. Although I promise you I am willing to compromise on that point. As for your beauty and charm, while they are considerable, they, too, are not my motivation, as I said." The frown became more genuine. "You mistake me, I think, for being a common sort of man. I do not love and wish to marry you *in spite of* your past, but *because* of it."

"Really." She had to sit down, with that. "You are right, that is not a common thought, and I confess I do not understand you, since such an opinion has never come my way before."

"I am sure. Any man until now who wished to offer you his hand or his, er, protection, must have had the attitude that your past would magnanimously never again be mentioned between you." At her nod, he said, "I, on the other hand, appreciate it. While it would disturb me to have the list of your former lovers named, or your affairs detailed, in general I have an enormous respect for a woman who, with nothing but her beauty and her charm--because, my dear, forgive me, but your acting ability is much better on the smaller, more personal scale, than it ever was on the stage--could win her way to a place in our society. More than win her way, in fact. Such things have been known to happen, after all. Men can often be counted on to be foolish. But you have *graced* our society. I have no idea how you did it, and would be most anxious to learn, but somehow you have altered your language, manners, and style in such a way that you have not only aped your social betters, but surpassed them. Contemplating this, and admiring it, was the first step I took toward falling in love with you."

Her astonishment was, if anything, only more profound. "I know not what to say!"

"I will take that as promising. Surely surprising you by not being a man of common mind must be helpful to my cause. I will warn you, I doubt but that I will make a devil of a husband. I am two score and four years of age, a lifelong bachelor, and set in my ways. As much as I appreciate your taste, I will object strenuously to having my home redecorated from attic to cellar. I am often abstracted in my writing to the point where I am able to ignore another human being in my home for days at a time. I am easily irritated, especially when interrupted while in thought. I am neither fashionable nor gregarious, and can be mercilessly rude to those whose minds are inferior."

She smiled. "These are faults indeed. And against them, what do you put on the scales to tempt me? What are your virtues?"

"I will love you until the end of my days. Even when you have grown old and lost your beauty, I will love and respect your mind, your heart, and your courage. I will challenge you, and I hope never bore you. I will make whatever compromises I must to assure that you are happy in my home."

"But you will be troubled by the disapproval of your family, maybe even estrangement."

"Good heavens, woman, surely you do not think that weighs with me! The only member of my family whom I hold in any particular affection is Georgiana, and she adores you. As for the rest, my attendance to my duty ends at once when my happiness is in question. My sister, my nephew, and anyone else who has objections they feel entitled to raise will do what they please, but not in my home or my presence, so I think we need not consider that. You see that I have skipped one of my faults, which is that I am a selfish man."

"You are also a frank one."

"Then I ask you to be equally frank with me."

"I will, sir." She thought for a long moment, and he remained silent. "Sir Henry," she said at last, "you are aware that I have found no uncommon delight in your company. I like and esteem you very much. But until this moment, I have not considered love or marriage, with you or anyone. I was quite settled and contented in my current state."

"Yet I have hope. You are considering it now, not rejecting it out of hand."

"Indeed I am. I must. You realize, I'm sure, that the warmth of my feelings toward you are not equal to your own toward me."

"I did not expect that. I only want hope that I can somehow animate them to that point. I will do whatever you wish toward that end, and naturally wait as long as I must for your answer, one way or the other."

"It is not in my nature to take long over a decision, even an important one. Nor would I torture any good man with such delay." She drew breath, her hands folded in her lap. "Should I decide to marry you, it will be because I believe I will come to love you as deeply as you do me. But at the moment, my mind is in confusion, and I must consider the issue in peace and solitude."

"Of course."

"I will call on you this afternoon at three o'clock, if you will be at home. I believe your sister is engaged for the military review at that hour with your nieces and a large party of friends. So without chance of offending her, I will come then and bring you my answer."

"So quickly?" He was both surprised and worried.

"I am a woman who knows her own mind and heart, Sir Henry. I am in confusion now, most unexpectedly, but once I am calm again, reaching a decision will not be difficult for me. I will see you then."

# Chapter 25

Georgiana did not go to the review that afternoon, her mother deciding that the sight of handsome officers in full regimentals would have a detrimental effect on her already questionable morals. Since her absence allowed the inclusion into the party of Miss Emily Atwell, whose small, pretty face had lit up at the very mention of it, before it fell again into apology and insistence that Georgie go in her place, Georgie was able to add the pleasure of a feeling of virtue to that of following her own inclinations. An entire afternoon in her mother's society, far from her uncle's benign influence, was not at all to her taste, and a military review would bore her. She would much rather stay at home.

She did not, however, read any of the illuminating and worthy books her mother informed her would enrich her time, but instead, as soon as the carriage was gone, ran downstairs to discover if her uncle could alleviate her solitary hours.

She found Sir Henry in the front drawing room, which was unusual enough, but even more peculiarly, he was sitting on the window seat, a book open at his side but unread, and in a state of some perturbation. When she asked him what was wrong, he denied any trouble and changed the subject at once. "Left behind, and bored, Georgie? Did you come to me to be entertained?"

"Yes, Uncle, but not if you are troubled or my presence is a problem to you. I do not want you to feel obligated to put aside your own thoughts for my entertainment."

"When have you ever known me to do so?" he demanded.

She had to smile. "Never before now."

"Nor do I now. Yes, there is something on my mind, but I welcome the distraction. Chess?"

"I might just win, if your mind is elsewhere," she smiled.

"Ah. Backgammon, then. Or cribbage."

She brought out the backgammon board, and with it, they whiled away half an hour or so. Her uncle glanced often at the clock on the mantelpiece, which stirred her normal curiosity to a fever pitch, but he made no explanation.

At three o'clock, she heard a carriage outside. At once, in mid-move, Sir Henry leaped up and went to the window, and his agitation became more severe and noticeable. "Georgiana. Go upstairs at once. Or down into the library, if you prefer. Remain there until I send for you. Now, at once, go."

She went upstairs swiftly, impelled by the urgency in his voice, but she stopped on the landing and knelt so that she could look through the banisters without being seen, as she had when she was a child, and could observe who was being shown in. To her astonishment, it was Lady Shipton.

In her bedroom, Georgie picked up the latest horrid novel, hoping its spine-tingling terror would alleviate her more real suspense, but for once the trials of the lovely, swooning heroine had no hold on her attention. Lady Shipton here, to call on her uncle--what did this mean? The thought that leapt to her mind, that Sir Henry planned to make Lady Shipton an offer, was rejected at once. He'd shown no sign of being infatuated with the lady, only an uncommon pleasure in her company, and he had none of the indications of a man either violently in love or even planning to make a change in his household. Yet what else would bring Lady Shipton here, where hitherto she had courteously but firmly refused to come? What else would throw her uncle into such a state of perturbation?

She cast aside the book and paced the room impatiently, but she'd scarcely made two circuits when a maid entered and said that Sir Henry requested her presence in the drawing room. She all but ran down the stairs, only recollecting her dignity when she saw the footman at the door. Then she brought herself down to a stately walk, lifted her chin, nodded politely to the footman, and pretended not to see his grin as he let her into the drawing room.

Sir Henry and Lady Shipton were before the hearth, hand in hand. Even as Georgie assimilated this, her uncle turned a beaming face on her and welcomed her warmly. "Georgie! Come in, come in. Please. It is entirely appropriate that you should be the first to wish me happy. Lady Shipton has just consented to be my wife."

Georgie was stunned, despite this having been one of the possible reasons she had been able to consider for Lady Shipton's visit. But once her moment of stupefaction passed, she was transported with delight. She flew across the room to embrace them both joyfully. "But, Uncle Henry, did you *want* to get married, after all these years?"

"Not at all, but Lily would not have me on any other terms," Sir Henry said, smiling fondly and with more animation than was his wont.

"Lady Shipton, you will be my aunt! Oh, this is by far the most exciting and wonderful thing to happen to me in London."

Lady Shipton, gracefully receiving yet another enthusiastic embrace, said, "I am glad it pleases you so, and since, yes, I will be your aunt, I hope you will call me Aunt Lily."

"It will be odd, but I will strive to, because it will give me so much pleasure. Uncle Henry, we must call Addison and have champagne brought!"

"In the middle of the day?"

"Aunt Lily, when you're married, you will try to make him just a little less stuffy, will you not?"

"I will indeed, and I think champagne would be a lovely thing to have at this moment."

"Say no more," said Sir Henry. "I shall have Addison fetch it at once."

While he pulled the bell, the two women sat on the couch, Georgie keeping a hold on both of Lady Shipton's hands. "Do you really love Uncle Henry?" Georgie asked.

"Do you not think he is lovable?"

"I think he's one of the most lovable men in all the world, but not everyone else does."

Lady Shipton turned her fine eyes on the trim figure of Sir Henry as he gave his butler orders. "I think you are quite right, Georgie. I think," she added, her voice becoming so musingly quiet that Georgie could barely hear, "that I shall be truly happy for the first time in my life."

Georgie squeezed her hands. "I am so pleased, for both of you."

Lady Shipton smiled. "Anyone can see that. And I noticed that *Aunt Lily* came very readily to you."

"Perhaps I have a second sight, and have been preparing for this event from the day I first met you. When will you marry?"

Sir Henry approached and said, "As soon as is possible. An announcement to the *Gazette* is already prepared and will be sent today."

Lady Shipton gave him an arch look. "You were very sure of me."

"I could always have burned it if you disappointed me." To Georgie, he said, "As to the date, we had not yet discussed it in any detail. Lily, do you wish to have banns posted?"

"Not unless you do. I can as easily be married by license. If you do not know a bishop, I know several."

Sir Henry laughed, in a way that Georgie had rarely ever seen him do. "I am not going to inquire into how you know them, my dear. But I do know one or two, and shall deal with that. Will your stepson be a problem, as far as settlements go?"

"None. My portion is all my own, neither in his gift nor his control."

"Then we'll give the lawyers a few days to draft everything up, and marry in a week. Does that suit you?"

"Eminently."

Georgie's eyes were huge. "A week?"

Sir Henry said, "You disapprove?"

"Oh, no, of course not! But Mama will be mad as fire!"

Lady Shipton turned stricken eyes on her fiancé, but Sir Henry's chin was set in a granite line. "Maria has no voice in this," he said.

"She is your sister," Lady Shipton quietly reminded him.

"Lily, we've discussed this."

"Still, perhaps if we waited until the end of the Season, when she returns to Rowland Hall...?"

"I have been waiting more than twenty years to find a woman I can tolerate in my life. I shan't wait another moment. And, Georgie, you do not object, do you?"

"Object? Except for the effect on Mama, I could not be more delighted or excited."

"What about Cecilia? This is her Season, after all," asked Lady Shipton.

"Cecy will be charmed," Georgie promised. "Where will you honeymoon?"

To her amusement, it seemed her uncle had given this no thought. He turned an apologetic face to his betrothed, who said, "I had an idea about that. I thought, perhaps, a week in the country would suit us both well. At

Rowland Hall, if your sister would not object, or, if she does, I'm sure James will allow us the use of Lakeford."

"You do not wish to travel? Paris, perhaps?"

"No." She reached out to touch his hand, briefly. "I am past the age where I need diversion. I would prefer a location where I can contemplate my good fortune, and learn to know you better, in quiet serenity. Besides," she added with sudden humour, "I already know how much you loathe travel, and am immensely flattered that you even made the offer."

"It went against the grain, but you know I'd do anything for you."

"Yes, I do know that. I shall take great care not to ask for anything I do not truly want."

As they smiled into each other's eyes, Georgie remembered something Richard had once said, *Of all people, lovers are the most tiresome with whom to be in company.* She began to see his point.

As if her thought had conjured him up, they heard a carriage stop in front of the house, and when Georgie went to the window, she saw Mr. Harding descending from his curricle. "It is Richard! Should we deny him?"

"No!" said Sir Henry. "Let him come in and share in the news. Although I doubt he will share in the joy," he added cryptically.

# Chapter 26

Before Georgie could ask what her uncle meant, Addison opened the door and announced Mr. Harding. Richard strode in, still wearing his caped greatcoat, although he'd left his hat with the footman. He was obviously expecting to take Georgiana for a turn in the Park, but stopped dead, startled, at the sight of Sir Henry and Lady Shipton, who were again holding hands across the space between the couch and chair. He made a quick recover, bowed, and was greeting Lady Shipton with proper address when Georgie cut him off. "Oh, do not bother with all that, Richard! Uncle Henry and Lady Shipton are to be married!"

Mr. Harding stripped off his gloves and shed his greatcoat, placing them all into Addison's hands, and said without any trace of surprise, "My congratulations to you both. I cannot imagine a better suited couple."

"Did you know this would happen?" Georgie demanded. "Because I had not the least idea."

"Your powers of observation have evidently been blinded by your prejudice."

"Prejudice! What prejudice is that?" she demanded.

"Why, that you see your uncle as you have always known him, as your uncle. You fail to see him as an individual and a man."

"Oh. Well, yes," she admitted sheepishly.

He bowed over Lady Shipton's hand, wishing her happy. Smiling up at him, she said, "I hope to wish you equally happy some day, Mr. Harding."

Georgie frowned. What did she mean by that? The idea that Richard might be considering matrimony was surprisingly unpleasant to her, for some reason. But her momentary concern was banished by his next words, which were spoken coolly.

"I thank you for the wish," he said, "although it is not likely. Sir Henry, my congratulations to you on your exquisite taste in women and your good fortune in securing this one. I confess, I had not thought you up to the challenge."

"I had inspiration. And not only Lily herself, but also my niece, who set me a fine example of courage."

"Me?" Georgie squeaked.

"Indeed. If not for your extreme valour in the face of overwhelming filial odds, I should never have met Lily."

"Oh, *that*."

Addison opened the door to a footman bearing a tray with the champagne and four flutes. Sir Henry poured, and the four of them toasted the coming marriage. Then Lady Shipton abruptly sobered. "Oh, my dear. How can we say there is no impediment to our marriage?"

"If you are going to mention Maria again...!"

"No. Something much more serious than that. Addison and Ardmore!"

Sir Henry paled. "Naturally, the salaries of both will be no problem, but the precedence will be... insurmountable!"

"Either one of them must give way, or one of us. I do not suppose Addison is ready to retire?"

"He will never be. And you would not like to lose Ardmore."

"He has been my strong right hand since my marriage to Shipton."

Mr. Harding said, "It seems to me that nothing could be simpler." All three of the others stared at him, and he said, "Allow me to explain. Sir Henry, am I right in assuming that money is not a difficulty?" Sir Henry, too wise to ask useless questions, simply confirmed this. Mr. Harding went on, "And am I not also correct in believing that Addison has been complaining for some time about how much he dislikes the City, and even the modest entertainments you hold?"

"Quite true, but Addison has always complained about those things."

"Then the solution seems obvious to me. Buy a house in the country. With a wife, this would be desirable anyway, especially in the summer. Addison would be content to reign there, and Ardmore here."

Sir Henry blinked. "You have not the longest of brains, Richard, but you are sometimes amazingly practical. I shall do so. It shall have to be handled with the greatest tact, but I believe it can be done. Lily, my love, we will have to support Ardmore in your own house until we find a suitable property."

"Of course! This is a delightful measure. I would love to have a home in the country, with my own garden. I have sorely missed Lakeford since Shipton passed away. Not that I was not welcome there, but that is not the same as it being your own home."

Georgie said, "Uncle Henry, you must live near us. There are some very pretty properties not far from Rowland Hall. Please, say you will!"

He glanced at Lady Shipton. She nodded, smiling. "Very well, Georgie," he said, "we shall at least enquire there first."

Mr. Harding said, "I will send word to my own man of business. He is local, and familiar with the area. He will find you a place which does not flood in the spring, and across which not even the most wide-ranging hunt will gallop."

Sir Henry laughed. "You know me too well. I will be grateful to you for your help."

"Call it a wedding present, since otherwise I shall be quite at a stand for what to get either of you." He rose. "And now, I am sure you will pardon me if I take Georgiana away. The two of you must be wishing us both at the devil."

Both Sir Henry and Lady Shipton protested, but Georgie knew that for mere courtesy, and went to get her bonnet and parasol.

In the curricle, unfurling the parasol, Georgiana at once demanded of Mr. Harding, "What do you think of all this?"

"This marriage? It shall be the making of both of them. But it will be most unpleasant for you."

"Why? I have not lost an uncle, I have gained a most delightful new aunt."

"I am thinking of your mother, of course, which you would know if you were not so jinglebrained."

"I have already been in her black books nearly this entire Season. Besides, surely she cannot be so prejudiced as to wish Uncle Henry not to be in love."

"I have never noticed that love figured greatly into your mother's estimation of a suitable marriage partner for anyone in your family, or that your uncle's happiness was for her a desirable end."

She was embarrassed, for he had spoken what she had been thinking. He made her realize, by stating it so baldly, just how unfilial she was. "You have never liked my mother," she murmured.

"I would like her very well if she did not persist in thinking me twelve years old, and would forgive me for allowing you to eat blueberries in your white dress."

She laughed. "Mama has long forgotten that, I'm sure. Why, that was more than fifteen years ago."

"I protest. Your mother's memory is far too good for her to have forgotten any of my misdeeds, never mind one so heinous as allowing you to get blue stains on white organdy." He looked down at her. "But nothing I ever did has been the equal of the way you have displeased her this Season, and I have no doubt she will make you suffer for this latest development. Are you very sure you do not want to marry me? We could have a double wedding, and Cecilia may come and live with us."

"That's very generous of you, Richard. Nor will there be any problem with the butler."

"None at all."

"But, Richard...." she began, and then stopped, blushing in confusion.

"You worry me. When you have something to say which you cannot simply blurt out to me, I become quite alarmed. What is it?"

"You shall consider it prying and impertinent."

"I doubt it. If so, I shall consider the source."

"How unkind!"

"There, you see? I have been unkind to you, so you need have no hesitation to say something I might not like."

She glanced up at him through her lashes. "I just wondered... did you perhaps wish to marry Lady Shipton yourself?"

He was so startled that the reins slipped in his fingers, and his horses picked up their pace for several strides before he got them in hand again. "*Me?* Wish to marry Lady Shipton?" he said with such evident astonishment that she had to smile.

"I guess not," she said.

"My dear girl, where in the world did you get such an idea? She's considerably older than me, to begin with."

"Not so many years. And you have often spoken of her beauty and wit. Besides, you are on excellent terms with her."

"That can be said of many ladies. Nor do I think this idea was in your mind until just now. What put it there?"

"Just something Lady Shipton said. About wanting to wish you happy, as well. And you were not quite yourself with my uncle. I doubt either he or Lady Shipton noticed, but I did."

"I doubt Sir Henry or Lady Shipton would have noticed if I had come in and stood on my head."

She giggled, but persisted. "Still, you were not yourself."

"If not myself, then who?"

She would not be put off. "Someone less warm and affectionate than I expected."

"Oh, that's quite easily explained. After having proposed to you several times and been so soundly rejected, I am bitter toward any man who has formed an attachment and carried it through to a happy conclusion. It took all my self-possession to wish them happy when I am not."

"I do beg you would be serious. If not Lady Shipton, is there someone else you wish to marry, but cannot for some reason?"

"You can ask this? You? If there were, do you truly think me cad enough to propose to you? What if you'd accepted me? A pretty pickle I would have been in."

"You would be anyway, if I took you seriously. Do stop fobbing me off, Richard," she begged, putting a hand on his arm. "If there is something making you unhappy, then I want to help in any way I can."

His smile warmed his face. "I assure you, I am not unhappy, Georgie. How could I be, with your friendship? Put it out of your mind. I think your imagination has run away with you, most likely because you dread the effect of this announcement on your mother."

"I hope that, after the initial shock, she will be happy for him. He is her brother, after all."

"Would you be happy if Charles married someone of whom you disapproved?"

"I would, if I thought she would make *him* happy."

"So you believe that happiness is the only thing to be sought in marriage?"

She pondered this a moment. "I suppose not. There are other things to consider, and after all, no matter what the circumstances, one cannot *always* be happy."

"Indeed, that would be uncomfortable after a while. Eternal happiness would be boring."

"Yet heaven is promised to be eternal happiness."

"Perhaps when we are dead, we might be able to receive it. As normal human beings, however, we must have our spirits tried with occasional lapses into irritation, anger, even tragedy."

"I maintain, however, despite all this, that happiness should be the first, primary consideration in a marriage. Do not, I pray, begin to tell me the other reasons why a person will marry. I know them all."

"But you do not approve of them."

"No, I do not. Some, however, I can understand, if not entirely approve. Such as in the case of Miss Vail, who married the curate."

"Security and comfort may be all the happiness that some people desire."

"Yes, but I thank God daily that such is not my situation. When I marry, if I do, it will be for love."

"A romantic notion, and quite worthy, but apparently difficult to achieve, since you have been three years on the town without, so far as I know, developing a *tendre* for anyone."

"It is a most lowering reflection," she agreed. "There have been many for whom I thought I might form an attachment, but they all came to nothing."

"Perhaps you, like your uncle, are hard to please, and you will not marry until you are four and forty."

"As if anyone would want to marry me then!"

"I sincerely doubt you will have to be concerned about it."

She looked up at him. "But what about you? You've been on the town *much* longer than I have. Will you be a bachelor all your life?"

"If you will not marry me, I suppose that will be my fate."

"What a depressing thought. If you reach four and forty without having found a woman who will make you happy, then I *will* marry you."

"Being married for the sole reason that I have reached a certain age will undoubtedly assure my complete happiness," he said dryly.

"I promise not to bring an inconvenient butler with me," she said, and had the satisfaction of making him laugh.

# Chapter 27

"Elroyd," began Mr. Harding in a portentous tone.

"Yes, sir?" Unflappable as always, the valet presented Mr. Harding's mulberry-coloured coat to him.

Mr. Harding slipped his arms into the sleeves. "I am going to do it today."

"Are you, sir?" Elroyd said blandly.

"Don't you take that tone with me."

"No, sir."

Mr. Harding sighed. "I mean it this time."

"So you have meant it, every other time."

"This time I shall ask her with complete seriousness."

"Of course, sir."

Mr. Harding let Elroyd finish the adjustments to the well-fitted coat, then said, "I will allow her no opportunity to think me to be joking with her. And if she still insists on misinterpreting me, I shall stand firm and insist that she hear."

"Very good, sir."

"So when I return, you may be assured that we will be preparing the house for a mistress."

"Excellent, sir."

"Either that, or I shall be putting a period to my existence."

"Not very advisable, sir, even under those circumstances," said Elroyd with no change in his calm inflection.

Mr. Harding refused to give in to a smile, but said soberly, "No, for then you would have to find someone else to *sir* to distraction, will you not?"

"I would not care for that, sir."

"Would you not?"

"No, sir. If you would permit me to say, sir, I have taken no small pleasure in my duties since I have come to your service."

"I am surprised. It is not as if I do you credit."

"But you do, sir. Short of Mr. Brummell, there is no more elegant man in town."

"You exaggerate!" Mr. Harding laughed.

"Only slightly, sir. There are some gentlemen whose figures are better than yours, but these are Corinthians, and not to my taste. You have no actual defect in form, neither in leg or shoulder, and nothing for which unusual tricks or methods of tailoring must atone. You do not impose upon my handiwork any unfortunate desire to decorate your person, and in fact your own judgment in waistcoats is not to be disparaged. Furthermore, although you can be, at times, most satirical, your disposition is in general a good one."

"Do not forget that I pay you a good wage."

Offended, Elroyd said stiffly, "To a person of my position, sir, the consideration of salary is indelicate, even vulgar, to consider."

"Sorry. I forgot that you are not a servant, but rather, an artist."

"If you will but look in the mirror, sir, you will see the proof."

Mr. Harding obediently did so, but said, "I wish you were artist enough to make me as handsome as Lord Shipton."

"If I may be so bold, sir, I must hazard a guess that, in choosing a marriage partner, Miss Rowland will not have appearance foremost in her mind, but rather be seeking someone with whom she can be comfortable."

"That's all very well," said Mr. Harding, taking his hat and cane, "but if Shipton can withstand one of her scolds and keep his sense of humour about him, then I have no chance at all."

He arrived at Grosvenor Street just in time to see his most distinguished rival coming out of the door of Sir Henry's home. Lord Shipton was not quite his usual pleasant self, however. He appeared, in fact, much harassed, settling his hat on his head with none of his jaunty air.

He recovered himself on seeing Mr. Harding, and bowed. Then, since (somewhat to Mr. Harding's disgust) he did not see in Mr. Harding a rival for Miss Rowland's attentions, he greeted him affably and warned him, "If you are thinking of visiting the family, this is not, perhaps, a good time."

"Let me guess. Lady Rowland has been informed of her brother's wish to marry."

"Yes, and why she should upend the entire household for it, I do not know! But so she has. I did manage to get a few minutes alone with Miss Rowland..."

Here he stopped and looked so conscious that Mr. Harding, with a calmness that belied the turmoil within his breast, said, "Alone? Put it to the touch, did you?"

Wryly, Shipton admitted, "I did. Did you guess my intentions, then?"

"It was inevitable. Miss Rowland is a gem."

"Beyond all price. And yet..."

"Like all gems, she has a cutting edge."

"Indeed she has," Shipton said, with a rueful grimace.

"So she rejected you?"

Mr. Harding's hopes were lifted, and then dashed, by the reply. "In round terms, yes, she did. But not irrevocably. She gave me reason not to despair. I shall try my luck again when Miss Rowland is less distracted and annoyed with circumstances within her family."

"If you do that, you will have to wait until the Season is over, and follow them into Sussex."

"You are not serious!"

"I am. Despite the presence here in town of Lady Rowland, it is Miss Rowland who is chiefly responsible for the firing off of her younger sister this Season."

"Good God."

"If you decide to come to Sussex, please consider yourself welcome to stay with me at Five Oaks. It is barely two miles by road from Rowland Hall, and I would be happy to receive you there," said Mr. Harding, mendaciously, but with a true feeling of virtuous magnanimity. If this was tempered with the frivolous thought that, if the fellow succeeded with Georgie, at Five Oaks he could shoot him and bury the body with no one being the wiser--well, no one need know. Although he could not help but think of how Georgie, were she not personally involved, might laugh at the fantasy.

Lord Shipton, unaware of the possibly grim fate that awaited him at Five Oaks, even if only in the imagination of Mr. Harding, was unreservedly grateful. "That is mighty generous of you! I hope it will not come to that, but if it does, I shall accept your offer gladly and do my best not to be the sort of guest you wish to Perdition in a day."

"No fear of that," Mr. Harding assured him, quite honestly. If Shipton were not a rival, Mr. Harding would have enjoyed his company very much.

Lord Shipton said all that was proper, made his bow, and made his escape. Despite the earl's warning, Mr. Harding went lightly up the steps to the door and was let in.

# Chapter 28

Georgiana was in the drawing room alone, and she bore all the marks of being in a most ill temper indeed. Since Lord Shipton was not so familiar with her, he might have been forgiven for not immediately noticing Georgie's faintly heightened colour, the few strands of wayward hair on her shoulder, and the slight downturn to her upper lip. All of these were warning signals as prominent as banners to Mr. Harding, who knew her well. With an inward sigh, he resigned himself to reporting failure yet again to Elroyd, although not quite yet to putting an end to his existence.

He certainly could not do that when Georgie so clearly needed him. She greeted him with outstretched hands. "Oh, Richard, you have no idea how glad I am to see you!"

"I can guess," he said, taking her hands in his and settling them both on the sofa. "I met with Shipton outside."

"Oh! Did he tell you his errand?" she asked with a slight blush.

"He did. And also that he did not prosper. Yet I thought you liked him."

"I like him very much indeed, but not enough to marry him. I hardly know him, after all. And if his behavior today is any sign of his general understanding," she added tartly, "then I know him well enough to refuse him again, should he ask."

"Did he offer you offense?" he demanded.

"No! Of course not. He was all civility and kindness. But honestly, Richard--before he even spoke, while we were still exchanging small talk, I told him something of what goes on here, and what a turmoil we are in. I confessed to him that I was quite distracted. So what does he do then, but launch into a list of all my good qualities, an avowal of his regard, and a proposal of marriage! Ridiculous! I ask you, would *you* do such a thing?"

With a wry recollection that he actually *had*, in fact, done just such a thing in Sussex, at Rowland Hall, Mr. Harding consigned honesty and Lord Shipton both to the devil and asserted, "I would not be such a fool."

"Exactly. I am naturally flattered by his regard and honoured by his offer, but how could I entertain the thought of such a drastic change in my circumstances at this time? How could I even *think*?"

Her voice had risen, and Mr. Harding's complacency over the foolhardiness of his rival was diverted to concern. "My dear girl, is it as bad as all that?"

"Yes," she said baldly, and to the astonishment of them both, she burst into tears.

Most men would have been taken aback, dismayed, and completely discomfited by such a blatant display of emotion and distress. Mr. Harding, however, was made of sterner stuff, and had moreover the advantage of having seen Georgiana weep before. He therefore unceremoniously put an arm around her, allowed her to wet the shoulder of his coat, and provided a handkerchief as soon as she'd regained enough of her self-control to sit up once more.

"Thank you," she said in a watery tone, using the handkerchief with vigor. "I cannot think what came over me."

"I can, and so can you. Do not be missish with me. We are too good friends, and I am entirely too familiar with the strains under which you labor."

"You are so kind to me." Another sob punctuated this statement, and she apologized again. "I shall be in control of myself again shortly, I promise you. But if you wish to leave, I promise not to blame you a jot."

"Leave you in such distress? I am not such a good-for-nothing."

"No, you are a brick." Under control of herself again, she offered him back his soggy handkerchief, and giggled at his revolted desire that she keep it.

"That's better," he said at the giggle. "Now tell me all about it. This is obviously not one of your mother's usual tantrums."

"It is not. I thought that, after the initial shock and her, er, natural reaction..."

"You mean a round of flat hysterics."

"Yes, unfortunately, such was the case. But I believed that, once she had her say and had time to reflect, she would accept the match. Of course I knew she would never be happy about it, and expected that she would most likely complain about it for some time."

"For some little time, yes. Surely not more than thirty years or so, however."

Despite herself, a gurgle of laughter escaped her. "Quite so. Oh, Richard, you are so good for me. I'm feeling less in despair already."

"And less in alt, as well, I see."

"Yes, and I do apologize for weeping all over you. I did not mean to."

"It is of no consequence. I am glad to be of use, and Elroyd will, I am sure, forgive you for spoiling this coat. Eventually. His complaints do not carry on quite as long as do your mother's."

"You are too absurd." Her smile wavered away again. "If it were just a matter of suffering Mama's abuse of my uncle and Lady Shipton, and her headaches and faintings, then I would not be so overset. But it is worse."

Since, despite his light manner, Mr. Harding had been considerably alarmed by Georgie's tearful outburst, he said, "She is not cutting off her brother, surely?"

"She was going to! I do not exaggerate. This morning she rose fully intending to end all intercourse with Uncle Henry. She declared that she had no brother, and was in the house of a stranger. A vile and depraved stranger, in fact."

Disgusted, he said, "You would think Lady Shipton was planning to fill the house with actors and Haymarket ware."

"Precisely. In fact, she said something about *high-flyers* and *bits of muslin*."

He started. "Excuse me, Georgie, but I never fail to be amazed at what your mother does not hesitate to say when she is in a temper."

"I know. It is quite shocking. Although you just now mentioned Haymarket ware, which is just as shocking."

"What is even more shocking is that you know what I meant! But do not try to split hairs with me. I assume you talked her out of cutting off Sir Henry entirely?"

"I did, but only after the strongest representations of the ills it would bring us."

"Not the least of which would be the substantial diminution of yours and Cecilia's dowries."

"That was the last thing of which I thought, but--and this is most lowering--it was the one thing which swayed her to reconsider. However, she is adamant that we are to remove from here immediately, or at least within the week, before the... the *corrupting* influence of the new Lady Becknall is felt here. I am so upset! To see my uncle so enraged and disturbed, and to have them brangling like a pair of children! Cecilia has taken to her bed and refuses to come out."

"Leaving all the care of your mother upon you."

"And upon Bridges, who has been of great help in calming her."

"But not, I deduce, of bringing her to a reconciliation to Sir Henry or acceptance of his new wife."

"No, not at all. Bridges is even more disapproving, if that is possible, than Mama is." She sighed. "I can say this only to you, but, oh, Richard--I was so looking forward to seeing Lady Shipton here with us, and seeing with my own eyes how my uncle looks when he is truly happy and not just contented."

"You will not be allowed to even visit?"

"I have been specifically forbidden to do so, and in no uncertain terms. Mama blames the entire thing on me."

"That is outrageous."

"No, not really," Georgie admitted fairly. "I did introduce them. Uncle Henry would never in the whole course of his life have met her otherwise." Her chin firmed. "But, no matter what Mama says, I am *glad* I did it!"

"As is Sir Henry, I am sure. Glad and grateful. My dear girl, you have nothing for which to reproach yourself. Your motives were of the best, and if the results have been both disastrous and blessed, then you must pluck up and accept both the joy and the vexation that inevitably attend the practice of excessive virtue."

"I admit, until now, speaking to you, I saw only the vexation and had forgotten the joy."

"Yet you say you will not be here in this house after the end of a week. Where does your mother intend to go? There cannot be an acceptable house to lease anywhere, not now at the height of the Season."

"She intends us to go to Rowland House, to Charles."

Mr. Harding stared at her for a moment. Then his eyes began to twinkle, and a few seconds later, helplessly, he began to chuckle. Georgie chided him and rapped his arm with her fist, but then had to join in, and the two of them enjoyed a long bout of mirth. Wiping tears from her eyes again, only this time tears of laughter, Georgie said, "Oh, you are too bad. You encourage me to a disrespect of all my elders."

"Charles is only your elder in years, not in wit, understanding, or wisdom. Dash it, Georgie, when was the last time you were in Rowland House?"

"I know what you mean. My brother is a little careless."

"*Careless?* Your brother has a bachelor's establishment that makes your uncle's seem like the Brighton Pavilion by contrast," he stated roundly. "The front rooms are all given to billiards and card tables, and the furniture has either suffered greatly from abuse or been replaced entirely with what is comfortable for Charles and his cronies. You will not be able to make it fit for entertaining in anything less than a fortnight, and then only with great diligence, good luck in the warehouses, and a huge sum of the ready."

"I know! I have represented this to Mama. But she says we must go anyway. Actually, to be more precise, what she said was that we must all bear up under the suffering imposed on us by my uncle's infatuation."

"Infatuated, is he? Does she believe him bewitched?"

"Literally! I do believe she could see Lady Shipton burned at the stake, and say it served her right."

"Does she really hope to influence Sir Henry with this tempest in a teapot?"

"She did at first. She was certain that, when he realized how much his family disapproved, that he would give up Lady Shipton. Which naturally only made things worse. Especially since she broached the whole subject over the breakfast table."

"By Jove! Has she utterly lost her wits? Ring a peal over a man before he's had his coffee?"

"It was not wise of her."

"It was daft. Sir Henry, I am sure, pointed out that, as a man of mature years and experience, he is capable of setting his own course."

"He said so, and Mama told him that was balderdash, and that, since he had scarcely set foot from the house in the past twenty years, he is the last person to know what is proper and correct in society. Which is untrue!"

Mr. Harding leaned back and crossed his legs. "So much for the opening volley. Did she then bring up the troops?"

"She did. She pointed out to him the inevitable reflection upon myself and Cecilia, that it would ruin all our chances for contracting eligible matches."

"A gross misstatement and a tactical error, given your company of just a few minutes ago."

"Oh, she will dismiss that. She will say that Shipton is no better than he ought to be, for accepting his stepmama with complacency in the first place."

"Yes, we all know that Shipton is the very model of a decadent, dissipated young buck," he drawled, drawing another giggle from Georgie. "What was Sir Henry's counterattack?"

"He said that any man who was stuffed shirt enough to refuse to consider either of his nieces for a wife, simply because their uncle had wed to disoblige his family, was too much a gudgeon to be acceptable for either of us. He paid us the very pretty compliment of saying that we would be honoured for our own selves wherever we went, no matter to whom we were related. To that he added that we have a number of dirty dishes in our family tree already, amongst whom Lady Shipton would seem, in comparison, like a nun."

Mr. Harding laughed. "A flush hit! That was a doubler. What, then, was Lady Rowland's next stratagem?"

"She then appealed to Cecilia and me, to support her in her protest and beg him to reconsider."

He winced. "An error which, I am sure, rebounded to no one's credit."

"You can imagine what I said."

"To hazard a guess, I should say you informed her that Sir Henry is an adult, answerable to no one, and perfectly capable of making his own decisions without recourse to two women under the age of one and twenty, even in so weighty a matter as marriage."

She smiled her admiration. "Well, I did so, but not nearly as well as you phrased it. But Cecilia! You should have heard her."

His brows shot up. "I expected her to avoid speaking by dissolving into tears and running away."

"She did, but not until after she declared to Mama that she *liked* Lady Shipton and wished my uncle to do whatever he thought would make him happy."

"That must have been a facer."

"It was. Not another word was said by any of us. Not a single word. I vow, the servants even tiptoed around us."

"As things stand now, I assume you are in the unenviable position of go-between."

"I must tend Mama, comfort Cecilia, attempt to ameliorate my uncle's quite justifiable anger, and arrange all the details of our removal from this house."

"Poor girl! Is there anything I can do?"

"If you would be so kind, would you take a letter to Charles, and take it yourself, so you can explain the situation to him? For he will not believe Mama to be in earnest, if I only write, and I am far too busy to see him myself without great inconvenience."

"Naturally. It will be my pleasure. And I mean that quite sincerely," he added wickedly. "I would not miss seeing his expression at learning this news, not for all the world!"

She giggled. "*Odious* man. I shall write immediately, and I do thank you!"

# *Chapter 29*

Lord Rowland reacted to the news with all the astonished dismay that Mr. Harding could have wished.

He immediately called on his family, despite having only just risen, staying only to be shaved and dressed. He pleaded with his uncle to put off the wedding until such time as Lady Rowland could be reconciled, or at least until the end of the Season, but in vain.

Balked, he spent a fruitless hour with his mother, attempting to bring her to reason and to prevail upon her not to disturb his happy bachelor's existence (although naturally he did not put it in quite those terms). He even offered to find her a lease house, an offer she scorned as impossible.

Finally, driven against the ropes, he flatly refused to allow the move (which he called "this invasion", a military term Mr. Harding would have enjoyed). His declaration brought on an excess of vapors, during which he was declared an unnatural brother and son, and called a profligate who was so selfish that, in order to spare himself a few weeks' inconvenience, would rather see his sisters dwindle into old maids.

He surrendered at this, being no more proof against a mother's outbursts than any other young man, but he did so with an ill grace.

"I think I shall go stay with one of my friends," he told Georgie later. "I would rusticate to the Hall, but not in the middle of the Season! Why, I'd never live it down."

"Indeed, you might wish to stay with a friend," she agreed after a short hesitation. "I can promise you that you will have no peace at home."

"I do not know why Uncle Henry should take such a bee in his bonnet. At his age, there can be no excuse."

"No excuse? Charles, he's in love!"

"Fudge! Stuff and nonsense! In love? How so? He's forty if he's a day, far too old to be talking of love. As for infatuation, surely at his age, the blood has cooled. Only rank obstinacy must hold him to this early wedding. He could very well put it off until July or August."

Georgie put her hands on her hips and glared at him. "Why should he do so? To suit your selfishness?" she demanded.

Charles took his leave shortly after, but not without the parting shot of telling Georgie she was a termagant and in some ways exactly like their mother.

Lord Rowland did go to stay with a friend, and Lady Rowland took over Rowland House entirely. The condition of the house and the changes which had been made since she had last visited were so appalling that they occupied much of her attention for some time thereafter. While she directed the cleaning, refurnishing, and rearranging, being a tremendous trial to Charles' servants, Georgie took over the task of escorting Cecilia on their normal round of morning calls. To Cecilia's pleasure, they did not neglect their uncle. Neither of them ever thought to mention this at home, however, and their groom also inexplicably failed to mention it in the kitchen, where Bridges might have gotten word of it.

Exactly on schedule, Sir Henry and Lady Shipton were married, and took themselves off to Five Oaks, having been forbidden the use of Rowland Hall. Mr. Harding had offered his home and even gone ahead of them to prepare his servants for their visit.

He stayed long enough to introduce Sir Henry to his man of business, and between them, they set in motion the search for a suitable country property for Sir Henry and his new bride. So busy and ultimately successful was he that Sir Henry quickly closed on the estate of Birchland, not eight miles away. Birchland was a tidy property, which, although lacking a home farm or extensive property, was situated in a very pretty park, with a smallish lake, a bluebell wood, and several excellent trails for Lady Becknall to enjoy her horseback rides. The house was not large, but entirely satisfactory to Lady Becknall, who planned to entertain only on the smallest scale while there, and the rooms, while not many in number, were large, spacious, and airy.

Lady Becknall spent most of the last few days of her honeymoon in drawing up plans for a flower garden, complete with rose arbor, and terraced lawns leading from the back of the house.

Georgiana, visiting them the day after they returned to town, was unsure what to expect after her new aunt had spent a fortnight with no other company than that of her uncle. She was concerned that Lady Becknall would be bored and even beginning to regret marrying a man who was proud to claim he had not a single romantic bone in his body.

However, her fears were laid to rest at once. Lady Becknall was blooming, and Sir Henry's disposition was altogether more lively and more *there* than ever before. The house on Grosvenor Street was already beginning to be altered, with vases of fresh flowers strategically placed, and curtains cast open to allow in more light. Sir Henry was not only accepting of the changes, but unconcerned with Lady Becknall's further plans for new furniture and a more modern kitchen.

Addison was not there, being already installed in state at Birchland, where he was as happy as it was possible for a man of his nature to be, taking great pride in managing the house in such a way that it would always be ready to receive Sir Henry and Lady Becknall at any time, with a moment's notice.

In Grosvenor Street, the servants were awed to complete cooperation by Ardmore, whose manner was more high in the instep than any lord's, and a French cook had been installed to reign over the kitchen. Mrs. Haycock might have taken exception to being so displaced, except that Ardmore pointed out to her that she had other duties more suitable to a housekeeper in a properly run gentleman's home, and such was his manner that she believed him implicitly.

Furthermore, as Georgie related gleefully to Cecilia in a *tête-à-tête* on her bed later, Uncle Henry had somehow found a romantic side to himself. His attentions to their Aunt Lily were tender. He had also given her, on their return to London, an emerald necklace that exactly matched her eyes, and he had arranged as a surprise, while they were in the country, to have his stables converted from storage back to their original use. All Lady Becknall's own carriages and horses were now installed there.

No one, Georgie vowed to Cecilia, could be as happy as the Becknalls.

"You will be some day," Cecilia said.

"I doubt it. I have passed all the eligible bachelors of London under my eye, and found them all wanting. Although there are one or two who will do for *you*," Georgie teased. "And once we have you married off, perhaps I will turn my attention to Emily."

Cecilia giggled. "I think that may already be in hand. Freddy Winborne has been ignoring me utterly lately, whenever I am in company with Emily. It is most uncivil."

"Then he must be in love. For you know the line--*Is not general incivility the very essence of love?*"

"I knew there was an apt quote, but I just could not recall. At all events, I expect an announcement any day now. And he is just the man for her. He's gentle and kind."

"And not excessively intelligent," Georgie smiled.

Cecilia gave her a mock scowl. "Oh, he would not do for *you*. But there is no defect in his understanding."

"You are quite right. But, Cecy," she said, sobering, "this will not do. I brought you to London to make a match for *you*, not Emily Atwell. Have you met any young man you can like?"

"Dozens!"

"I mean, that you can like enough to marry."

"No," Cecilia admitted. "Doubtless I will end up being as hard to please as you are, and end up on the shelf."

"*Cecy*!"

"I did not mean that you are on the shelf! No, I did not, so stop laughing. But you should not chide me, for you have seen and met and even been courted by more gentlemen than I, and you have not yet met one that you like."

"Not well enough to be legshackled to him," Georgie agreed, with more feeling than propriety of language. "Not even Lord Shipton, and he seemed so promising at first. Handsome, of good breeding and excellent manners, charming--and he loves Shakespeare. Truly, what more do I want?"

"You want to be in love. Cannot you be in love with him? Mama would forgive you all, if you became a Countess."

"I cannot be in love with any man who quails at my slightest frown," Georgie laughed.

"Surely he did not! Georgie, you are unfair! I know you better, and I am sure that you put a flea in his ear, the poor man."

"If a mere *flea* sends him running with his tail between his legs--!"

"It did not! You are too hard," Cecilia said, but she was giggling, too.

It seemed to Georgiana that there was only one man in the country who did not fear her occasional tongue-lashings, and that was Mr. Harding. But despite his several proposals of marriage, the thought never once entered her head that she might marry him, or that he seriously wished to marry her.

She was allowed to continue in this belief until the day after her appearance again at Almack's after the long absence enforced by her mother. Mr. Harding was there, and during the waltz, he asked her if there might be a chance he would be able to see her alone the next day, as he had something particular he wished to ask her. Even then, she was oblivious to the possibility. She told him that she would be alone between the hours of one and three in the afternoon, as her mother was taking Cecilia on a duty call, something Georgie would be glad to forego.

# Chapter 30

The next day, promptly at one, Mr. Harding presented himself at Rowland House, looking quite point-device in the mulberry coat that, despite her tears, she had not been able to ruin past Elroyd's ability to mend. She greeted him with such sparkling vivacity that he at once guessed, "I think you have good news?"

"Very good. Pray sit down, and I will tell you. Would you like some refreshment?"

"No, I thank you. Do not keep me in suspense. Wait, let me guess. You are in such good looks, there are only two possibilities."

"And they are?"

"One, you are in love."

"Wrong. Guess again."

"The other, that your mother has somehow been brought to see reason."

"That is it!" she crowed.

He put a hand over his heart, pretending to be staggered. "I do not recall feeling an earthquake, and I cannot imagine that anything less would attend such an event. Who performed the miracle?"

"Lady Jersey! She saw Mama this morning on Bond Street and stopped to talk, and told her how pleased she was to see me at Almack's last night. They fell into conversation, and when Mama began to complain, Lady Jersey said how entertaining she found Lady Shipton, and that Mama would be foolish to allow the world to see her make such a fuss over so trivial a matter. Mama did not dare contradict Lady Jersey, and the end result is that she is now saying that perhaps Uncle Henry's excellent morals will set a good example for Aunt Lily, and she is telling everyone else that we removed from Grosvenor Street solely in order to give the newly married couple some privacy."

"I am all admiration for your mother. Such social adroitness! Like a cat, fling her as you will, she lands on her feet. But this must be excellent news for you."

"Indeed. I am no longer an unnatural child, I will have you know, although I am still too willful for my own good. Mama has not yet bent enough to give me and Cecilia permission to call on Uncle Henry, but I believe she soon will. So all is well with us at last, and I can openly rejoice in Uncle Henry's happiness."

"I am glad for you. This has been a difficult Season for you in every way."

"Yes, and I am no closer to finding a husband for Cecilia than I am for myself."

She was about to add that she felt as if she had neglected Cecilia's interests in the most shabby way, except that she was forestalled by Mr. Harding, who rose and paced to the window, saying, "Well, as to that... It is about that I wish to speak to you."

She was completely baffled. But he was obviously in earnest, so she ventured, trying not to sound either astonished or amused, "You wish to offer for Cecilia?"

The moment she said it, she got the most queer sensation. But she had no chance to analyze it, because Mr. Harding turned with a sound of disgust.

"Honestly, Georgie, for a girl who uses her brain more than most, you sometimes have more hair than wit."

"I... what?"

"I want to offer for *you*, you paperskull!"

Exasperated at such ill-timed humour, she began to protest, "Richard, do not start--"

But again, astonishingly for one so courteous, he interrupted her. "Start what? Joking with you?" He visibly collected his wits and said bitterly, "I suppose I deserve this. Had I not been such a coward at Rowland Hall, you would never have fallen under such a misapprehension."

"Misapprehension?" She was stunned, and certain she could not be understanding him. "Surely you do not mean to seriously offer for me!"

"I did then, and I do now."

"Impossible!"

He glared at her. "Why impossible? We are male and female, of a proper age, not related, and without any familial impediment."

"But... you do not truly want to *marry* me!"

"Yes, I do! What in the world must I do to convince you of that fact?"

"You want to marry *me*?"

"Have you windmills in your head? Have I not said so? In fact, have I not said so several times?" he added with understandable anger.

She still could not believe her own senses. "Why?"

"I told you that in Sussex." He had always been reticent about his feelings, if they were strong, so it was with an effort that he said, "I told you then that I loved you. I meant it."

"But you have always considered me a sister!"

"I have not thought of you as a sister for a good many years now."

"I do not... you gave me no indication your feelings had altered."

"I intended to," he admitted wryly, "but I felt it unfair to take advantage of our long acquaintance and marry you before you had so much as set foot in town. So I determined to wait until you had your first Season. And after that, the time never quite seemed right. Especially since, during your first Season, you made it plain how much, how very much, you depended on my friendship. I did not want to take the chance of destroying our relationship, so I continued to hesitate and find excuses for not formally offering for you."

"Until now."

"My patience is not infinite, and my nature has never been altruistic." He drew a breath. "Take it as a measure of how much I value our friendship, that I was so loath to hazard it, I waited two years to make my proposal."

She felt as if something inside her were fracturing, leaving a void. "We can no longer be friends as we were," she whispered.

"But we can be more!" he said, taking a step toward her.

She put out a repulsing hand. "No. I cannot... you must see this is impossible."

"We have already gone through that discussion. Impossible is not the right word."

"I cannot think of another!" she said, completely mind-shattered. "I have always been used to thinking of you as a brother and a friend. I cannot change that. I am unable to think of you as a husband."

"Unable, or unwilling?"

She swallowed. "Unable."

After a moment of appalling silence, he bowed with dignity. "Very well. I am, of course, sorry for it, and am also sorry that my declaration will inevitably affect the close friendship we have hitherto shared. However, I thank you for your honesty, and, once a suitable interval has passed for me to master my disappointment, I assure you that you may still rely on me as you always have."

"Richard, I never meant to bring you pain."

"I acquit you of that, and I am sorry to have been the cause of any pain to you. My feelings are fixed, and will not change, but I will never mention this matter to you again, nor hope for any change in yours. I have many reserves for resignation, and I promise I will not pine. You may be comfortable." At the door, he turned. "My very best wishes for your continued happiness, Georgie," he said, and was gone.

Georgie sat staring at the closed door in a total fugue of shock. Richard, in love with her? Wanting to marry her? Richard, whose heart she had always been sure was no more susceptible to romantic love than that of her uncle's?

But her uncle *had* fallen in love. And so, apparently, had Richard.

Ardmore entered to ask if she wanted refreshment. She rose, told him no, and pushed past him to run up the stairs, pleading a sudden headache. In her own room, she threw herself on her bed and burst into tears of grief and shame. She had treated Richard abominably, had hurt him, and, worst of all, had lost her best friend forever.

# Chapter 31

Georgie told neither her mother nor her sister what had passed between herself and Mr. Harding, and used her headache, which had become real after a prolonged bout of weeping, to avoid the pleasures planned for that evening. In the morning she went down to breakfast much more composed, but still heavy-eyed and listless.

Cecilia was alone at the breakfast table, and remarked on Georgie's looks. "You do not seem at all the thing. Is this my fault? I know how much strain my come-out has put on you, although I might not seem to."

"No, Cecy. I'm simply out of sorts, and will be well shortly, I am sure."

"Your headache must have been dreadful. I know when I have one like that, it puts me on end for another day entire."

"That is mostly likely the case, and I will be myself again tomorrow," agreed Georgie, pushing her food around her plate.

"I hope so. You look terribly pulled."

Rallying herself, Georgie said, "Never mind me. How was the ball last night?"

"You surely do not want to hear me chatter on about a ball."

"On the contrary, I think that is exactly what I need the most. Tell me who was there, and who you danced with."

Cecilia obliged, at first hesitantly, then warming to the subject. She was still young enough that every ball was an adventure, especially one in which she had been so sought after. "Lord Shipton stood up with me," she said, "but talked only of you. I am sure he will ask you to marry him again. Will you turn him down again?"

"I believe so, but never mind that. Was Mr. Winborne there?"

This was a successful diversion, for Cecilia at once went into detail of the very great attentions Mr. Winborne had paid to Emily, which included dancing twice with her and taking them both down to supper. Listening to her merry, inconsequential chatter, Georgie slowly relaxed and even began to feel less low.

Then Cecilia said, "I saw Richard as well, but he was in a foul mood. Not that he was discourteous, but you know how he can get, with his eyes all frosty, and so satirical there is no bearing with him. But when I asked what had put him in a bad humour, he denied it. Maybe it is just that he must go out of town."

Georgie dropped her fork. "He is going out of town?"

"Yes," Cecilia said, unconscious of the effect of her words. "Some trifling matter of business at Five Oaks which requires his attention. Although," she added, a line appearing between her brows, "he did say it was possible we would not see him again in town for some time. I told him that would be a great loss to us, and particularly to you, but he said that, since Mama was reconciled with Uncle Henry, he believed he might venture so far as Sussex without inconveniencing you. You know his way."

"Yes," agreed Georgie.

Cecilia, who was often more shrewd than anyone realized, asked, "You two did not quarrel again, did you?"

"Nothing to signify. Why do you ask?"

"No reason. Only that both of you are acting oddly at the same time, and Puddles says that he left here yesterday in the very deuce of a temper."

"Surely you know better than to listen to kitchen gossip."

"So you did not quarrel?"

"No, of course not."

"That is good, for I like Richard. I never used to--he used to quite frighten me when I was a child."

Georgie smiled at her. "You have gained a great deal of self-confidence since coming to town."

"Have I? Yes, I suppose I have," Cecilia said, pleased.

"You have, if Richard's critical ways and ill humours no longer put you out of countenance."

"Why should they? He has always been underfoot, as long as I can remember." She did not notice Georgie's wince at these words, but went blithely on with what, to her, were much more interesting topics of conversation.

Georgie had no intention of telling anyone about Richard's serious intentions toward her. But she ended up telling her uncle and aunt, not of her own volition, but because, on seeing her listless spirits, her Uncle Henry guessed the cause.

"Did you *know* he was going to offer for me?" she asked.

"I did. We spoke of it once."

Georgie turned to her aunt. "Aunt Lily, did you also know? You do not look at all surprised. Did he tell you his intentions?"

"No, he did not. But I assumed it, from watching his behavior with you."

"I do not understand. What was different in his behavior?"

"I cannot say that anything was different, since I never observed him in your company before this Season. But it was plain to me, seeing the two of you together, that his attachment to you was a strong one. When with you, his expression was completely different than when he was with any other young woman."

"In what way?" she faltered, not sure she wanted to know what was meant.

Lady Becknall hesitated, choosing her words. "His manners are always good, of course, but with you, he never seemed the least bored. And he was also more tender, more lively, and always with a smile ready to appear."

"To all of which," Sir Henry said, "my niece was apparently blind."

"I was," admitted Georgie. "We have been friends for so long, I never really looked at him." She raised her eyes to her uncle's. "Do you think he truly loves me, or is this just a passing fancy?"

"Do you want the truth, or some consoling words only?"

She wilted. "I know your answer already, then."

"If it is any consolation to you, he is not the kind of man to go into a decline because he is crossed in love. I am sure that, after this repairing lease at Five Oaks, he will be able to master his emotions enough to become your friend again."

Lady Becknall stared at him. "Henry, would you have been able to do so, should I have refused you?"

"Yes, of course I would have."

"How? For I will not believe your love to be less deep than that of Mr. Harding."

"I would have forced myself do it, for my own sake, and for yours. For yours, to keep you from the distress at having caused pain to another. For my own, to allow me the solace of your continued company."

"In other words," said Georgie, "having failed to gain Aunt Lily as a wife, you would have accepted half a loaf as better than none at all?"

"A starving man will take what he can get," Sir Henry said gently.

"That is not right," Georgie declared. "It is offensive, in fact."

"Is it? I am sorry to have offended you."

"No, I do not mean that. You have not. I simply cannot accept such resignation."

Lady Becknall hid a smile and said, "What would you have him do? Throw you over his saddlebow and gallop off with you to Gretna Green?"

"No, do not be absurd. But..." She gestured helplessly. "Richard deserves better. I do not know how to face him again! I cannot help but think it will be cruel to do so."

"You will have to," Sir Henry pointed out, "since his ties to your family are so close. Unless, of course, you plan to marry someone else and move far from Sussex."

"Someone like James?" suggested Lady Becknall.

Georgie said stiffly, "I am highly honoured by Lord Shipton's feelings toward me, ma'am, but I cannot return them."

"That is a pity. I would have loved to have you as a daughter as well as a niece. But you must make your own choice. Georgiana," she said seriously, "I have sampled marriages both of convenience and of love, both of which have been happy. But I do not think I have to tell you which is the happiest state. I would not have you marry for any reason other than that you are in love. While I think it a pity that you do not prefer James, and am surprised that you do not love Mr. Harding, since the two of you seemed so well suited, I would not ever wish to encourage you to settle for anything less than what I have found with your uncle."

For some unaccountable reason, this speech made Georgie want to weep. In a choked voice, she said, "I thank you. I do not think you need fear that."

"I am glad."

Sir Henry said, "But do not discard Richard's friendship out of consideration for his feelings or awkwardness for your inability to return them. That would be doing him a disservice."

"I think it would be more kind."

"Not at all. If he truly loves you, as I believe he does, he will take joy in being of service to you. He is far too rational to think, as some young men might, that if he persists, you will eventually accept him, so you need not fear any renewal of his offer. You are a sensible and caring girl, Georgie. Do not deny him the right to be your friend, simply because he was so bold to ask for more."

"He did say that was why he never spoke until now, because he feared losing my friendship," she admitted miserably.

"Then be kind, cease being embarrassed, and allow him to keep your friendship."

"I do not know if I can!"

Lady Becknall and Sir Henry exchanged enigmatic glances at this, but said nothing. Sir Henry patted Georgie's shoulder and said, "Well, you will do your best, I am sure," and then changed the subject.

# Chapter 32

The remaining weeks of the Season passed in a blur for Georgie. Richard did not return to town, and she missed him greatly. She regretted daily her insensitive disregard of his feelings when she had rejected his offer, and although she knew that sheer surprise had occasioned her unintentional cruelty, she was still ashamed.

At last, with her uncle's advice in her mind, she summoned the strength of mind to write him a letter. This effort took some hours and a great many crumpled sheets of paper before she was able to find the right words, both to apologize for her behavior and to assure him of her continued regard, without wounding him further. She signed it, *Your friend,* and posted it quickly, for fear that she would turn coward and never mail it if she did not.

A week passed with no answer, and by the end of the week, she was so eager to receive the post that Cecilia wondered aloud from whom she was expecting a letter that was so important. At last, eleven days after her epistolary effort, her reward came in a letter addressed in Richard's distinctive, sloping handwriting. She took it from the servant with a calm that was excessively hard to maintain and set it aside without reading it at once, since she wished to give away nothing to either Cecilia or her mother. As a result of this determination, she had to wait many hours before, at last, she was alone and could hastily break the seal and read the words.

*My dear Georgie* were the first words her eyes settled on, and she released a startlingly heavy knot of pressure in her chest with a long, happy sigh. He did forgive her. She read the rest eagerly, and quickly, for it was very short. As a letter, it was much like any of his others, the only thing of real interest to her being summed up in the first paragraph, where he said, with all his usual satirical humour, that she had nothing to apologize for, as he understood her feelings completely and was quite accustomed to her moods, so had taken no offense at her manner when last they'd spoken. He then said his business at Five Oaks would most likely keep him in the country for another few weeks, but that he was looking forward to seeing her and her family when they returned to Rowland Hall. He sent polite greetings to her mother, Cecilia, and the Becknalls, and closed with, *Yours*, the only other thing in the letter which could even remotely be considered affectionate in any possible way.

Georgie was hugely relieved by this. She was convinced, now their breach had been healed, that she would be able to meet him again with ease, and that someday, perhaps very soon, they would be back on their old footing and comfortable again.

This complacence did not endure, however. She had told her uncle and aunt about what she had written, and she visited them that day to tell them of his answer. Sir Henry and Lady Becknall were both pleased with the result, and praised both of them as being rational creatures who would resolve this sticky issue in the best and happiest possible way.

Rather than feeling gratified by their praise, however, Georgie felt flat and dull. When she got home again, she took the letter from her dressing table drawer with the intention of consigning it to the fire. Instead, she sat and read it through once more, and yet again. She was discontented by it, with no clear reason for her discontent. She should be glad that his heart was not broken. Had he sent her a letter full of despair and declarations of undying love, she would have hated it.

She had not lost his friendship, for his words, satirical as they were, gave a clear signal that he had every intention of resuming their relationship as it had been before that unfortunate incident. He was the best of men, and she was an ungrateful wretch. She at once sat down to write another letter, to tell him so, but threw it away without posting it. What use was there? She would see him soon enough. Before she did, she must somehow compose her mind so that his generosity of mind would be met by an equal generosity in hers.

This, however, turned out to be more difficult than she thought. She could not forget his words when he'd proposed, or the anger in them when she had asked if he actually meant he wished to marry her. He'd almost shouted back at her, "*Have you windmills in your head? Have I not said so? In fact, have I not said so several times?*"

Such anger from him could only have come from frustration, humiliation, and pain, all of which, unknowingly, she had forced on him. Yet how could she have known he'd meant all those proposals?

Thinking about him now reminded her how much she missed his company every day. She had no one with whom to laugh at the more preposterous things she saw and heard in society, no one who fully shared her keen sense of the ridiculous. She had no one now to talk her out of a bad temper or relieve her frustration when her mother began to despair of Cecilia's ever getting a respectable match, and blamed it all on Georgie's bad influence having made her sister far too particular. Nor could she forget how kindly he had offered her his shoulder to cry on when her cares had become too heavy for even her strength.

As Uncle Henry said, she could have Richard's friendship again. Richard had said it himself, although recalling his words--"*...once a suitable interval has passed for me to master my disappointment, I assure you that you may still rely on me as* *you always have*"--made her want to weep more than rejoice. No strength of will that she possessed would ever bear her up under knowing she'd hurt him so much.

As the Season dwindled away, Georgie did not lack for partners or admirers, but they seemed insipid to her. They wished to treat her as a delicate blossom or a fine lady, without knowledge of her spirit and courage, and without the wit to admire those qualities even if they had seen them. She finally came to a point where the only company that did not bore her was that of the Becknalls, and even that was spoilt one day when Lady Becknall said, quite casually, "Georgie, you recall Miss Hazleton? You met her when you attended the party at my old home. I was wondering--I would like your opinion. Miss Hazleton is a bright, vivacious girl, and I thought she might do for Mr. Harding."

"For Richard?"

"Yes. Obviously he is ready to take a wife, something for which a man must be fully prepared before he attempts to gain one. If he should like Miss Hazleton enough to marry her, then you may be completely comfortable in his happiness, and lose that little awkwardness you must naturally feel now. Henry, what do you think? Should we invite Miss Hazleton to Birchland next month?"

"I have no objection. You know that any friend of yours will be more than welcome to me."

Georgie lifted her tea cup and said casually, "Why is such a worthy young woman not already married?"

"Oh, that is quite simple. She has the reputation of being a bit of a bluestocking. She is not, in fact, but she is well educated and well read. Another point in her favor with Mr. Harding, do you not agree? For an ignorant girl would disgust him. He is not like other men, frightened away if a young woman has a mind and opinions of her own, and Miss Hazleton is spirited and has an excellent sense of humour. I think they will suit admirably."

"I think you should not be matchmaking," said Sir Henry, amused.

"I will not do anything so vulgar. I shall simply introduce them. In London, such an introduction would go almost unnoticed, but in the country, where the company is so much more restricted, they might be thrown together quite often, and he will certainly notice her more."

"But the man just broke his heart over Georgie here," Sir Henry pointed out, still amused.

"Then Miss Hazleton can help him mend it. What do you think, Georgie?"

What Georgie actually thought would not have been polite to divulge, and in fact were the most uncharitable thoughts she had had of anyone recently, never mind her much loved Aunt Lily. Richard, to be considered so shallow that his heart could be mended in a moment by a girl who was a stranger to him? Yet, at the same time, she realized that Aunt Lily was correct, and that a spirited, intelligent, humourous girl was exactly the kind of girl who would appeal to Richard.

A girl, in fact, much like herself.

That was when her heart finally opened to her. The very thought of some Miss Hazleton coming to Sussex and stealing Richard away from her filled her with a hot wrath that would have astonished that young woman, had she ever known about it. Miss Hazleton! Who was Miss Hazleton, to go to Sussex and in a few weeks of society, convince Richard that he did not love Georgie at all? What had ever come over Aunt Lily, to imagine that the affections, which had been years in growing, could be blown away like a feather by some other comely and available female?

So shaken was she by her anger at this intervention by her aunt and by the sheer effrontery of the unknown Miss Hazleton at ever thinking she could have Richard, she answered her aunt's question and all subsequent conversation completely at random. She excused herself as quickly as she could, but refused her uncle's offer of a carriage. She had to walk, both to cool her burning cheeks and to think about why she was reacting like such a shrew to her Aunt Lily's well meant gesture.

# Chapter 33

When Georgie had gone, Sir Henry turned to his wife and asked, "Who, might I ask, is Miss Hazleton?"

"Oh, I made her up. She does not exist."

He gaped at her. "But you spoke of her as if you knew her well!"

"My dear Henry, I am an actress, after all! Or I was."

He stared at her another moment in stunned astonishment, then his eyes lit with laughter. "You vixen. Laying a trap for our Georgie, are you?"

"Not a trap, no. Simply a nudge to help her understand her own heart. All this talk of *friendship*!" she said scornfully. "I do not blame you for such foolishness, naturally. You are, after all, merely a man."

"Thank you," he said humbly.

Not deceived by this meek behavior, she laughed and kissed him. "I am nevertheless sure I am right. Friendship is all very well, but it was the very issue which was creating a wall before Georgie, through which she could not see. A woman in love needs passion, even if only the passion of jealousy."

"So, in effect, you induced her to throw her heart over that wall, with the hope that she will then jump after it."

"If it worked, that will be wonderful. And if not, then there will be no harm done."

"There will be one unfortunate result."

"What is that?"

"Georgie has a retaining memory. She will expect you to produce this Miss Hazleton and bring her up to scratch."

"Oh dear. I suppose I shall have to let a consumption carry the poor girl off," Lady Becknall said airily.

Georgie was walking home, filled with all the jealous passion for which Lady Becknall could have hoped. She had barely turned the corner, however, before she realized how foolish she was being. Why should she be contemplating horrible fates for a Miss Hazleton whom she had never even met, much less knew well enough to believe her deserving of being boiled in oil? Why should the image of a Miss Hazleton putting her white fingers on Richard in his mulberry coat, or even his blue one, make her think of vultures?

She stopped, so quickly that the person behind her actually bumped into her and passed her with an apology that she never even heard. For just a moment, she had listened to her heart, and her heart had said in no uncertain terms, *Richard is mine. Mine!*

No one else could have him. His life was hers, and hers was his. They belonged together, forever. Their lives had always been together, and their affections bound to each other.

*How could I have been so stupid?* she berated herself, walking on blindly. *I, who pride myself in my intelligence and understanding?* She had mistaken her heart. In fact, she had ignored it utterly. She had preached to Cecilia about falling in love and marrying for love, and all the time she had been in love herself and never even known it. Yet when the chance came to marry the man she loved, what had she done? Laughed! And then scorned it. There was no woman in England as stupid as she.

She knew Richard well enough--better than anyone else!--to know how difficult it must have been for him to hazard making her an offer, not just once, but many times. She would not put him through that again. She would tell him directly that she had been wrong and did want to marry him. If only he would listen!

She was trying to find words, thinking up pretty speeches and then discarding them at once, even as she walked up the steps to Rowland House. She went straight up to her room, tossed aside her bonnet and pelisse, and, being the kind of girl to whom action naturally followed decision, she found Miss Puddleforth at once and told her to pack for them to go at once into Sussex.

"Into Sussex, Miss Georgiana? But why? Is there a problem?"

"A very large problem, but not one over which you need concern yourself. I daresay we will not be gone many days. No, wait. You cannot be spared here. Find one of the maids to accompany me."

"You are not going with your mama?"

"No, nor with Cecilia. This is not their affair. I must handle it alone. Go, please, and make arrangements. Send a message around to Bloomsbury that I will need our traveling chaise. Oh, no, he must have gone to Five Oaks with Richard. Dash it!"

"Miss Georgiana!"

"Never mind. Send a footman to tell whoever is in charge of Mr. Harding's stable that I want the traveling chaise sent here at once, and that the postboys should apply to my Uncle Henry for charges and a sum of money for a night on the road, if needs be."

Miss Puddleforth frowned at her. "What is this start, Miss Georgiana?"

"I cannot tell you now, Puddles, but I will eventually. Please! It is of the utmost importance! I must leave at once."

"You should wait for your mother to return."

"If I do, I shall never be able to leave. You know that. I shall write her a letter while I wait. Will that satisfy you?"

To her dismay, at that moment her sister walked into the room. "Cecilia! Is... is Mama home as well?"

"No, not yet. I left her at Lady Bidwell's, and a proper bore that was! That mushroom of a cousin of hers was there, and I could not bear it another moment. Mama loves to be toadeaten, but not me, so I said I had promised to go shopping with you, and made my escape. Why in the world do you look at me like that? And what is the matter with you, Puddles?"

Georgie pushed Miss Puddleforth from the room, reminding her of her orders, then turned to Cecilia and said, "You will think I've run mad, Cecilia, but I must go back to Rowland Hall at once."

"Are you?" Cecilia exclaimed happily. "Are you going to reconcile with Richard?"

Georgie stared. "What do you know about that?"

Cecilia turned to her dressing table and picked up Mr. Harding's letter. "You left this lying open and in plain sight, so it is not as if I was prying. I was able to guess what he referred to, quite easily."

"You were?"

"I am not so long in the head as you, Georgie, but I am not stupid! It is as obvious as a toad in a bandbox that he is head over ears in love with you and has been for a long time, and you with him." She impulsively wrapped Georgie in an affectionate embrace. "I am so glad you finally realized it! Let us get packed, and we will go at once."

"You are not to come with me."

"You cannot go alone!"

"I will take a maid. No, Cecilia, my mind is set. Your own pleasures should not be put aside for days, simply because you have a most silly sister. Besides, if you go, too, then Mama will follow."

"Oh. Yes, I see. Very well, I will stay behind and make your excuses. When you return engaged, Mama will forgive all."

Georgie sat down on her bed abruptly. "If I do return engaged. Cecilia, you have no idea of the terrible things I said to him."

"Phoo!" said Cecilia, snapping her fingers. "*That* for whatever you said. I am sure Richard cares nothing for any of it. I have heard you berate him like a fishwife, and heard him laugh at you for it. You see from this letter that he is quite himself! Just go, and throw yourself into his arms."

"As if I would do anything so improper."

Cecilia giggled. "Richard will not think it improper at all."

# Chapter 34

At noon the next day, Mr. Harding, who had no business at all to conduct at his home and was therefore about to perish with a combination of boredom and bad memories, took himself off to his garden with a volume of Shakespeare. The agonies of the Bard's famous Dane would, he trusted, take his mind off his own troubles for a few hours.

With a casual disregard for his clothing, which would earn him reproaches later from Elroyd, he sat on the ground instead of one of the benches. He chose the shade at the base of a large oak, one of several that crowned a hill from which he had a pleasant view of the countryside. Stretching out his long legs, he settled down to the oblivion of reading, and if the fair Ophelia took on the features of quite another young lady in his mind, and if he took some petty satisfaction in the image of Miss Rowland mad and drowned, that was quite understandable in the circumstances.

For despite the easiness of his letter in reply to Georgie's, he was far from reconciled, and was in fact so bitter that the letter had taken him a full three days to compose. Sir Henry misjudged his nature, for it would be long before Mr. Harding would be willing to accept his half-loaf, and he was sure he would never be happy about it. His sole comforting thought was that Georgie might marry someone who lived in Yorkshire or even Scotland or Ireland, and be forever out of his sight. The sooner the better, as well.

He thought nothing of it when he spotted someone at the base of the hill until he saw it was a lady. Even then, he did not realize who it was until she was halfway up, and he did not quite believe his eyes when he did recognize Georgiana.

*She has come to apologize in person*, he thought, and could not help the warmth that he felt at the depth of her heart. Like it or not, he would have to make her believe he forgave her, and make her comfortable again. He could do no less.

He watched her approach as she crested the hill, her cheeks flushed with the exertion, one hand holding onto her flat-crowned straw hat with its pink ribbons flying over her shoulder in the wind. Although he kept an expression of disinterest on his face, he could not help but take pleasure in the picture she presented. She was not a diamond of the first water, it was true, and she was of average height when tall and slender was the fashion, and dark when fair girls, like Cecilia, were in style. None of this mattered to Mr. Harding. He saw only perfection, and felt only joy at the smile in her eyes, which was just for him.

But he would be dragged behind wild horses before he let her know it. "Georgie, what the devil are you doing here?"

"I was about to ask you the same thing. This is a long way to go, just to read a book," she pointed out, stopping before him.

"You will not object if I do not rise."

"No, not at all. I am accustomed to your rudeness. You will not mind if I sit down? I am quite out of breath."

Hope leaped within him, but he stifled it. This was how she would act if she were just come to apologize and reassure herself that he did not hold a grudge. "A little climb has done you in? By all means, then, sit down. I am sorry I have no cape to spread for you, to protect your skirt from the grass."

"I would say that shows little foresight, but you did not expect me." She sat beside him, her smooth arm brushing his sleeve, her scent borne to him on the light breeze, and her curls tickling his chin as she pulled off her hat and fanned herself with it.

"I did not expect you," he agreed. "Are you all come back from town early? Does this mean you have succeeded in finding Cecilia a husband?"

"No, nothing like that. Mama and Cecilia are still in London. I came back alone, and just for a day or two."

"Whatever for?"

"To see you, naturally. Before you met Miss Hazleton."

"Who the devil is Miss Hazleton?"

"You have not met her yet."

"That has already been established," he said impatiently. "Who is she, and why should I be meeting her?"

"My aunt thinks she will suit you." When he only stared at her, she clarified, "As a wife."

"Devil a bit! Since when does Lady Shipton--I mean, Lady Becknall--play at being a matchmaker? And why for me?" he added in high dudgeon.

She giggled, wrenching his heart. He'd always loved her giggles. Their merry music had never failed, until now, to lighten even his heaviest mood. "I do not know why Aunt Lily is matchmaking, and I do not care," she said. She settled herself against the bole of the tree. "Do you know, I have been doing some thinking lately on the manner with which matches are made in our society. And I think there is a certain injustice about the procedure which should be addressed."

"Perhaps at the next meeting of Parliament?" he asked dryly.

"Perhaps."

"And what is this particular injustice that so exercises your mind?"

"It is the inequality between the treatment of men and women. If a man wishes to marry a woman, he has merely to ask for her hand. His is all the risk, it is true, but think of the fate of women. If they wish to marry a man, they are only allowed to hope that he will ask. Hope is a woman's only choice. She cannot even let him know of her feelings by flirting, or she will be considered fast. I think that it would be more fair if a woman was allowed to make an offer to the man of her choice, as well as the other way around. Do not you?"

Her tone was light and teasing, but nevertheless, his heart was pounding. "That sounds perfectly reasonable to me," he said, "but then, I am more rational than most men. I fear it will never make it to the floor in Parliament."

"I was not actually all that concerned with making a sweeping social change," Georgie admitted, looking down at her hands, clasped on the ribbons of her hat in her lap. To his delight, a blush was colouring her cheeks and throat. "I was thinking in a more personal manner."

"Were you?" he asked casually.

"I was." She swallowed. "Richard... when last we spoke, I was not myself. I have always prided myself on being flexible, able to accept change, even welcome it. But I did not demonstrate that quality then." She glanced quickly at him, but seeing no encouragement on his face, went back to studying her fingers twisting in the pink satin of the ribbons. "So I came to Sussex to see you, and to tell you that, now that I have had time to properly adjust my mind, I have realized that you are the only man in the world who can make me happy. In other words, I love you very much, and *not* as a brother, and I would like to make you an offer of marriage." She swallowed convulsively and, still without looking at him, said, "Will you consider it?"

"I do like this new custom of yours," he remarked. "I hope it becomes the fashion."

She looked at him, her eyes flashing. "How many women do you want to propose to you, then?" she demanded.

He laughed. "That's my Georgie. I was beginning to wonder who you were, for a moment there."

"Oh, Richard, you can be so provoking! Just answer me, yes or no. Although if you say no, I shall consider myself very unfairly used, because you said your feelings were fixed and would never change."

"Do not throw my foolhardy words back at me," he begged.

"They were not foolhardy!" she blazed, and then her face fell ludicrously. "Were they?"

He set aside his book and smiled at her. "I told you then that you sometimes have more hair than wit. I will accept your most flattering offer, Miss Rowland, with great pleasure."

"Oh, I am so glad! I was afraid I would have to resort to Cecilia's suggestion."

"And that was?"

"To fling myself into your arms."

He cleared his throat. "That would not be an unpleasant alternative," he admitted. The next moment, his arms were filled with soft, vibrant womanhood, a pair of warm arms were around his neck, and eager lips were lifted to his. Reprehensibly, he took full advantage of what was offered, and proceeded to kiss his beloved until she was breathless.

The next half hour was spent blissfully, with the kind of conversation that only lovers can find interesting, such as "When did you first...?" and "Why did I ever...?", punctuated by such gestures of affection as came naturally to them. This was followed by yet another half hour of more practical discussion. With Georgie on his lap, his arms around her waist and hers draped on his shoulders, they discussed where they would honeymoon and what changes would be needed at his residences to accommodate a new wife.

After enjoying himself with images of Georgie in his home, Mr. Harding recovered some of his presence of mind and his usual *sang froid*, and asked,

"Does this mean that your Mama will expect us to take Cecilia to town next Season and find her a husband, my love?"

His love, who showed a gratifying pleasure in being so addressed, said, "Certainly she will. After all, have I not proven myself to be the very best matchmaker in all the world?"

Mr. Harding, laughing, had to agree to a truth so self-evident.

The End

**You can find ALL our books up on our website at:**
http://www.writers-exchange.com

**All our romances:**
*http://www.writers-exchange.com/category/genres/romance/*

**All Catherine's Books:**
*http://www.writers-exchange.com/Catherine-Dove/*

# About the Author

Fantasy writer Kathy Ann Trueman also writes romance under the name of Catherine Dove. She lives in rural Texas with a lifelong friend and a menagerie that includes horses, dogs, cats, and birds. She's addicted to chocolate, dragons, books, movies, and football. She's a 50+ single who graduated from a small college and still prefers the quiet of country life.

An avid reader, she was an Army brat who spent most of her young life moving, so books became her most reliable friends. Her favorites are fantasy, science fiction, romance, and mystery, but she'll read almost anything, even cereal boxes if nothing else is handy.

Kathy's short story, The Sow's Ear, was published in Marion Zimmer Bradley's Sword and Sorceress anthology series.

Keep track of all her work on her author two pages:

**Kathy Ann Trueman:**

http://www.writers-exchange.com/Kathy-Ann-Trueman/

**Catherine Dove:**

http://www.writers-exchange.com/Catherine-Dove/

If you enjoyed this author's book, then please place a review up at the site of purchase, and any social media sites you frequent!

## *If you want to read more about books by Catherine Dove, they are listed on the following pages...*

# The Rowland Sisters

{Regency Romance}

*For the daughter of a gentleman during the English Regency, life can be a whirlwind of parties, balls and outings--all to catch a suitable husband. For Georgiana and Cecilia Rowland and their friends, finding and securing the right husband is further complicated by misunderstandings, prejudices, rebellion against social restrictions, uncooperative suitors...and sometimes their own wayward hearts.*

## Book 1: Mr Harding Proposes

Eligible bachelor Mr. Richard Harding has his heart set on marrying his lifelong friend and neighbor, Miss Georgiana Rowland. However, the two have been good friends for so long that, when he finally screws up his courage and proposes to her, Georgie thinks he's merely teasing!

Georgiana has good reason to be so distracted. Her younger sister is about to be launched into society and most of the work and worry falls on Georgie. Also, despite her mother's furious command, she's befriended the scandalous Lady Shipton, which brings both blessing and chaos to the Rowland family and to their kind uncle, Sir Henry. Worse for Mr. Harding, Lady Shipton's charming stepson takes a strong liking to the beguiling Georgie.

Mr. Harding keeps proposing, again and again, while still trying to support Georgie in her trials. Is it possible for such a good friendship to turn into love?

Publisher: http://www.writers-exchange.com/Mr-Harding-Proposes/

## Book 2: The Lazy Bachelor

Mr. Peregrine Tyndall has often been called the laziest man in London. Even still, stirred to the enormous task of matchmaking when a hunting accident suffered by his cousin makes him realize he stands in real danger of inheriting an earldom--with all its tedious responsibilities. In his opinion, the perfect girl to marry his cousin and give the earldom another heir than himself would be their childhood friend, Portia Freestone.

Mr. Tyndall doesn't know what formidable obstacles lay before him in this endeavour. However, when he joins a house party at the earl's country home with this match on his mind, everything seems to go wrong. In the first place, his normally obliging friend Portia has a secret. She has no wish to marry the earl--she likes him very well but the man she secretly wishes to marry is Mr. Tyndall himself. An even bigger problem is Miss Frances Armitage. She and her little sister Eleanor had been left in his guardianship, a duty he has benignly and completely neglected up to now. A furious Miss Armitage is about to descend on Lakeford Hall to demand that Mr. Tyndall take up his duties to her and her sister in a responsible manner--even if she has to force him to do it!

Publisher: http://www.writers-exchange.com/The-Lazy-Bachelor/

**Coming Soon**:
**Book 3: Cecilia and the Rake**

# The Wynters Series

{Regency Romance as Catherine Dove}

*Harriet and Sebastian Wynter are the children of a pair of archeologist explorers who traveled throughout the Mediterranean. Their childhood was filled with adventure, education, and even occasional danger, and they grew up to be brave and resourceful. With their parents' deaths, however, they are raised to adulthood by their beloved aunt in London. To please their aunt, they try to fit in with London society, but their love for adventure is always just beneath the surface, ready to launch them into trouble.*

**Coming Soon:**

**Book 1: Harriet Disguised**

Harriet Wynter is struggling to be a proper lady. She is successful, but she pays for it with frustration at her lack of freedom. When her brother goes off with some unknown stranger who claims to have a trunk that belonged to their late parents, she is irritated because he won't take her with him. But when he fails to return, she determines to rescue him, disguises herself as a boy, and sets off on the stage to follow his trail. Her resourcefulness will be tested as she faces kidnappers, smugglers, social ruin, and, most of all, love.

In a convivial evening with his best friends, Lord Ashurst drowns his sorrows with too much drink and passes out. His friends play a trick on him and set him, peacefully snoozing, on the next stage south. To his confusion, he ends up on a country road, without valet or horse or even a change of clothes, along with a young boy apparently running away from school. It doesn't take him long to discover the boy is actually a young lady, but he's captured by her courage and decides to help her find her brother. Harriet leads him on his first real adventure...

Publisher: http://www.writers-exchange.com/harriet-disguised/

**Coming Soon:**
**Book 2: Sebastian Undercover**

Sebastian Wynter returns from the Battle of Waterloo with a limp and a depression that even visiting his sister can't quite lift. He goes to the country home of his uncle, where he spent the summers of his youth, expecting to find peace. There he meets Eugenia, who is so shy he almost never notices her. His boredom is relieved by an old acquaintance, Payne, who'd once kidnapped him, years before. He joins Payne under cover to bring down a ruthless French pirate. He is aware of the extreme danger to himself, but never expects it to reach Eugenia. When it does, his feelings for her change his life.

Eugenia Slade has secretly loved Sebastian Wynter since she met him, when he went off to war. But she's an orphaned relative of his uncle's second wife, hardly more than a servant, with no beauty, no money, and a tarnished name - what chance does she have with him? She's too shy to even talk to him, and his only interest in her seems to be a mild pity. However, when she believes he's in danger, she finds her passion and courage run deep. Not only does she risk her life to help him, but when he learns to love her, she is willing to give him up for his own good.

# Greenspell: A Fantasy Anthology

{Fantasy as Kathy Trueman}

In this collection of fantasy short stories all featuring female protagonists, you'll find diverse, imaginative tales, including:

- A sorceress unravels a spell and gets a result she could never have expected...
- A young girl wins a contest--her prize: to speak with a god...
- A vampire in hiding fears she'll be blamed for the reckless depredations of another of her kind...
- A minstrel travels with a witch who has a pair of very unusual cart horses...

As a bonus, this anthology includes "The Sow's Ear", originally published in Marion Zimmer Bradley's acclaimed Sword and Sorceress series.

Publisher: http://www.writers-exchange.com/Greenspell/

# Stories from the Vale

## {Fantasy as Kathy Trueman}

*Generations ago, ships full of refugees from a vast war accidentally blew into a narrow, sheltered harbor between the cliffs of two mountain ranges. The people called the vast and fertile valley beyond the harbor the Vale and settled there. The Vale was also home to wild animals, dragons, and magical creatures called elves...and magic.*

*As the years passed, humans with no actual magical talent came to be born with a Gift-- a single ability. Among the Gifted, only healers are widely accepted, but for others fear and distrust has led to prejudice, persecution, and even murder. Although elves, humans and dragons essentially live in peace together, the nearly immortal elves are intent on preserving the Vale's isolation from the rest of the world. At any cost.*

## Path of the Dragonfly

Shak is anything but a simple soldier with a clear-cut mission in life. He's consumed with the relentless need for revenge against a man who was once his best friend. But that obsession is far from his only. Shak can't forget he'd abandoned two helpless children during a battle. Though the deed that he can't forgive himself for happened in the past, far from changing, he can't get past it...until his grandmother, a witch, offers him the chance to redeem the dishonorable act.

Those same children he'd left to their fate are in dire straits. To rescue them, he must travel to the mysterious and treacherous Crystal Valley and then find a way to get them back where they belong. Further complicating his life, the Crystal Valley holds a secret that threatens two armies, and Shak alone can save them. With an unequivocal mission staring him in the face, he discovers his enemy is close by--actually following him--and vengeance could at last be his.

At a crossroads, he has no choice but to determine which task he'll undertake... and which to give up forevermore.

Publisher: http://www.writers-exchange.com/Path-of-the-Dragonfly/

## Gifts of the Elven

The Vale is home of The Gifted, those born with magical talent that manifests in unpredictable ways that many look upon with suspicion and fear. Even as the Vale's king works hard to teach citizens truth and tolerance concerning the gift of magic, the process is slow and politically risky. Many of the Gifted have no choice but to seek shelter in the stronghold city of Safehold. But is safety possible even there?

Sixteen-year-old Arlin is a nobleman's son, grandson of the king of Vale. Handsome and spoiled, he was born to warrior parents with older siblings who outshine him in every capacity. Misunderstood, his sullen attitude alienates his family. With the sudden appearance of wings on his back--a very rare and visible magical Gift--Arlin has no choice but to, literally, take flight to protect himself and his grandfather's reputation as an impartial judge of Gifted rights.

Fiella was adopted as an apprentice to the local bookmaster, where she discovered her passion for books and talent for sales. Her parents were killed when she was only seven--an event she witnessed that led to her desperate regret and longing to help others. While traveling on her first book-circuit as a journeyman, she impulsively offers to help Arlin get to Safehold, a sanctuary for Gifted, not realizing the danger she'll be placed in by doing so. Not the least of her worries is the secret she's been carefully hiding: She, too, is Gifted.

Shonwin is heir to the lordship of Kuturan. When he was a child, his father was murdered by his own wife. Living with a mercilessly cruel parent led to Shonwin's single-minded devotion to Kuturan. When the king heard of the ruthless horrors practiced there, he tore away their income and livelihood, denying them the rights other lords of the land were entitled to. To rebuild his heritage and birthright, Shonwin means to have his revenge. Arlin's Gift will enable him to not only discredit and disgrace the king but strike at the king's protection of the Gifted and his own beloved grandson, Arlin.

Publisher: http://www.writers-exchange.com/gifts-of-the-elven/